# The Brooklyn Leprechaun

## Bernadette Crepeau

**Outskirts Press, Inc.**
**Denver, Colorado**

Outskirts Press, Inc.
http://www.outskirtspress.com

ISBN: 978-1-4327-5103-6

Outskirts Press and the "OP" logo are trademarks belonging to Outskirts Press, Inc.

PRINTED IN THE UNITED STATES OF AMERICA

*Dedicated to the Staff and Volunteers*
*of the*
*Office of Head Start*

*Administration for Children and Families*

*Because of your hard work and dedication, millions*
*of children and their families, have been given a fresh start in life.*
*Thank you!*

# Acknowledgments

Without the help and enthusiasm of the following friends, family, authors, artists and editors, this book would never have been written and a life-long dream would have been denied Thank you!

Anna Cottle, Brandie Minshull, Brittney West, Bunny Minshull, Charity Heller, Dorothy Churchill, Greg Ballard, Helen Wild, Karin Miller, Karli Clift, Laura Meehan, Liz Pollock, Lynne Borden, Mary Carlson, Pat Schaller, Peggy Rolf, Sally Smith and Suzanne Johnson and the wonderful ladies at Grammy's Used Book Store.

I especially like to thank Barbara Lancaster, international artist extraordinaire, for the beautiful cover.

# Interlude

 From his perch, high above the ancient ruins, Mick watched as the fog rolled in and with it, his constant nightmare returned. Fog so thick you could taste it on your skin, just as it was on that fateful night hundreds of years ago. He was once again laying in wait, and could hear the crew's laughter reaching shore, long before the galleon was visible. Another successful haul for Grace, the self proclaimed pirate Queen of Ireland.

Kidnapped and ransomed by a woman. Mocked by his peers, pitied by his servants, Mick had waited a long time for his revenge. His breath quickened as his mind replayed each event, the surprise of the drunken celebrants, his crew hauling the cherished booty to his smaller faster sloop, his drink from the jeweled flask of what he believed to be prized wine. He shuddered with the memory.

———•◉•———

"Thought I might find you here My Lord", Padraig said as he materialized next to Mick.

"Is it time then?"

"Nearly so."

"I am not in favor of this, tis as if I am offering up a young women to slaughter."

"Aye, as you have said. Let it be as is, My Lord. There is no other way.

*Chapter 1*

# Brooklyn

"I still don't know why we have to fly out of Newark, of all places, and why so late at night?"

"We only have an hour to wait until we *board the plane* to London, sounds real classy don't it?" I struck a snooty pose, threw my hip out to the side, removing my imaginary monocle and in my best English butler voice said, *"My dear friend, we are off to Ireland with a change of planes in dear old London town."*

Here I'm acting like a fool as if my fear of getting on a plane for the first time didn't make me want to lose my lunch. My silliness worked, Mary smiled.

This is all so incredible but we're tired. There's been so much to do to get ready to leave for this two-week vacation. It was a great adventure until we began to travel. We left Brooklyn at 4:00 p.m. The subway ride to Grand Central was crazy.

Mary wore her oversized backpack, carried a suitcase, and rolled another suitcase so large it could hold a small child very comfortably. I also had three pieces of luggage that I'd picked up at Goodwill. They didn't match, but at least they held everything I thought I would need, which turned out being my whole wardrobe. I included my work clothes; suits, skirts, dress shirts, and sweaters to mix and match. I don't own many clothes, but the ones I have are all top of the line: Valentino, Juicy Couture, St. Johns, and others I got at consignment shops at a great price. The business outfits I figured I could wear to meet the lawyer and any business people. There were also some casual jeans for driving around. Yup, just about everything I owned.

After the subway ride, we hauled our suitcases up a very long flight of stairs and walked the length of four city blocks to wait for a bus to Newark, New Jersey. Finally, at the airport, we found ourselves running through the terminal so we wouldn't be late.

When we finally arrived at the gate and showed our tickets, a bright and cheerful attendant said, "I am sorry but your flight has been delayed to 11:30."

Mary glared angrily at the attendant, "Whatsthematterwithyou? It says right on this ticket that the plane leaves at 9:30." She said, pointing to her ticket.

"I am sorry Miss; may I help the next person in line?" she said, looking past Mary.

Mary stomped off, threw her bag against the wall and sat next to it on the floor since there were no seats available in the gate area.

I really didn't blame her for being upset, but what can you do? We won the tickets. We at least got to fly free, even if we had to go to Outer Mongolia to get the plane.

I stood next to Mary and nonchalantly slipped out of my heels. Mary had plugged in her IPod and closed her eyes signaling that she needed time to zone out. I leaned against the wall and thought over all the events leading up to our rush through the airport.

It's hard to believe it was only a few weeks ago. Mary came home from what I thought was a meeting at the company she contracts with. Her long blonde hair was loose and windblown; I could tell that she had raced up the four flights of stairs. When I saw that Scarlett Johansen cocky smile, I knew she was up to something. She had not smiled very often since her Mom died two years ago after a year long struggle with cancer. Now she was like a whirling dervish as she waved tickets in the air and danced around our small studio apartment.

"You will never guess what, we're going to Ireland. Can you believe it, *we won the contest.*"

"We won a contest, what contest, I don't remember entering anything."

"You didn't, I did, and we won. I just picked up the tickets at the radio station. We're *going to Ireland!*"

I argued that there was no way we could afford the time off work. She argued back that her job only needed Wi-Fi access and she could do her work testing software, and wasn't I just working a temp job that I could leave with a two week notice.

Of course she won, hey what could I do? We both needed the break. The past couple of years have been hard. We hardly partied anymore, I don't remember the last time she had a date, not that I have had that many myself. Mary is either working at her computer or working on that Si-Fi book she is writing. I miss the laughs and why not, the flight is paid for. Even if we still have all the other expenses, I knew I had to take this opportunity. I really want to find out what's up with the lawyer, why the heck she stopped writing. I haven't heard from her in ages. It would be great to get all of that inheritance stuff settled; I still worry that they will say I owe back taxes or something.

———⊂«(●)»⊃———

"First, its rush rush rush…and now we have to wait? Unbelievable!"

"Hey this whole trip is something of a miracle, what difference will another hour or two make, heck we can use the rest."

"You're right about the miracle part, first I find that old jingle, and then the same day I hear about the contest on the radio. What are the odds? I enter the jingle in the contest, knowing it didn't fit into the times, I mean you wrote it when we were in the third grade when kids were dying with plastic bags, but today "beware, beware of plastic bags for when your child is near. Beware, beware of plastic bags they may be the death of the year" doesn't really rate with the lead poisoned toys and stranger danger we have now. How did it win the grand prize out of what I imagine were thousands of entries? It's just unbelievable!" Mary said with a puzzled look, as if she was still trying to figure out how we won the contest.

"Well your Mom always said never to question fate, but you have to wonder…"

"It could turn out to be the best thing anyway." Mary said. "When Mom died you took it pretty hard, even worse than I did somehow. The news of the inheritance cheered you up a bit. It seemed to give you some feeling of connection that you'd been missing all these years, with no family around."

"You and your Mom are my family but it would be great if I find some family over there. I never thought much about my dad's family or even about being Irish, except on St. Paddy's day, but then everyone is Irish on St. Pat's" I laughed. "I don't know but somehow inheriting the land in Ireland seems to me that somehow I'm connected to a family, even if there is no one left. Know what I mean?"

I moved aside my bright red Jimmy Choo's and joined Mary on the floor.

"Sure I do but your obsession with all things Irish since then may drive me crazy, but seeing you excited about something these days is worth it....I think."

"Yeah, I remember all the time I spent reading every Irish book the library had to offer, and harassing the librarian to order the ones I'd found online that they didn't carry."

"It's surprising that they didn't take your card away."

"I know, I did go a *little overboard*." I grinned.

"A *little* overboard, if I have to watch 'Darby O'Gill and the Little People' one more time I swear I'm going to scream. If it wasn't for this contest, I would've sold my last possession to ship you off to Ireland!"

"Then thank goodness for this contest."

"Even though I think you went a little crazy, some of the movies gave me quite the urge to go see the place myself. At least this way I get to go with you."

"I'm happy we're going. I'm worried about that land I inherited. You know you never get something for nothing. I wonder how much I owe in back taxes. I asked Maureen but she never answered; I wonder why she stopped emailing me. I haven't heard from her or anyone else in that law firm of hers in months. That's just so weird."

"You know Mom would tell you to cool the worrying. Thank

goodness she is not alive to hear you stressing out or about those nightmares."

"Sorry I woke you up again, I think it was something about being hunted and having to keep running." I was out of breath when I woke up, but that was probably from all the screaming. I wish they would stop. Maybe they will after the whole 'owning land' thing is settled.

Mary stifled a yawn and pulled out her travel list for Dublin. When Mary's Mom took me in twelve years ago after my dad died, I didn't think I would ever get use to living with them. It helped that Mary and I both attended Sister Mary Francis's third grade classroom. It was hard at first, especially when Mary pulls her 'alone time' stuff. I first thought her stopping in the middle of a conversation to zone out, just plain rude. But I have come to understand that it's just the way she is. Maybe she has the right idea, I will look over my list and it will help me keep my mind occupied while I wait. I have so many questions; I hope we find some answers on this trip.

—◦«◊»◦—

Now boarding rows 14 -28." announced the flight attendant.

We stood to join the line forming to board the plane. *I wonder if we're the only two people in the crowd who have never flown before. Everyone looks so calm.* I looked over at Mary and noticed that she no longer looked tired. In fact, she's glowing. I can just feel her enthusiasm and joy. It was coming from her in waves.

Mary's blonde hair hung down her back in a ponytail and her glasses had slipped down the bridge of her nose. Her casual look of jeans, T-shirt, and fleece jacket looked so comfortable; she fit right in with the seasoned travelers.

I wish I had thought to wear sneakers. They would've been so much more comfortable. Darn it, I saved for months for my Jimmy Choos, and I plan to wear them every chance I get.

We were in a tunnel thingy; I guess this was the loading ramp I'd watched them pull up to the plane when it landed. It didn't seem like we were moving very fast, or was I just excited to be finally beginning our journey. I smiled as I watched Mary. Normally she would've been pushing her glasses back up in a hurried, no-nonsense way, but now she just looked around. I knew that others felt her excitement as well, for several people looked at her and smiled.

I wondered what I looked like. I knew from the 'What to wear for springtime in Ireland' web site that I would fit right in with my gray, light wool-blend vintage Chanel suit and my new red shoes. I felt happy, excited, and scared silly. I couldn't stop the lists in my head. God, I sure hope I have everything I need. Do they even have stores in Ireland? Of course they have stores, what am I thinking. All I have ever seen is pictures of country-side, sheep and pubs. But they must have stores.

"Hope I don't look a wreck when I get there." I reached into my new Coach satchel that went great with my new shoes and checked my hand mirror.

"*Oh, my Gawd!*" I exclaimed.

"Mary, I look like a raccoon! Why didn't you tell me?"

Mary, who never bothered with makeup, just looked over at me and laughed. I had outlined my eyes in Summer Sky blue shadow to set off my suit. That had mixed with my Barely Black mascara and perspiration to create circles around my brown eyes. I quickly dug out tissues from my bag and repaired the damage.

While I was at it, I pulled out a handful of hairpins and put my wild brown hair into a French twist.

Finally we were at the plane. We showed our tickets to the stewardess, and she directed us to our seats. She has to be kidding me, I thought.

"How do they think they can get this plane in the air? It's huge! It must hold at least five hundred people," I asked Mary as we looked around us in amazement.

Our compartment of the plane had at least thirty rows, and each row had two seats on either side by the windows and a middle row of twelve seats. We were lucky enough to get two seats by the window, and we were nice and cozy. That's until the screens in front of us started with the instructions for what to do in a crash. This smiley, perky blonde with not one hair out of place, announced how to breathe into an oxygen mask, put on a life vest, and slide down a ramp to a rubber raft.

"*Ohmygawd* Mary, we're flying over an *ocean*, what were we thinking?" I asked nervously.

"Hey Bridge, it will be okay, they haven't had a plane go down in years or we would've heard of it."

I looked at her, but she didn't look much calmer than I was. Now I know why I heard they sell a lot of booze on planes.

"Mary, what's that noise?"

"Beats me, it sounds like a hamster running around in a cage, or mice squeaking."

"You think they oiled everything?"

"Bridge, did they announce where this plane came from? I mean we saw it land and it wasn't very long before they let us board. But they must have checked out everything right?" she asked hopefully.

We grabbed each other's hands and held on tight. I'm sure we both were trying to remember all the prayers we've ever been taught.

We talked for over an hour before we could wind down enough to relax. Even though Mary told me again all of the wonderful things she planned to see in Dublin, I still didn't have the heart to tell her that we needed to drive directly to Mayo first. She had left the budget and arrangements up to me, and I just couldn't figure out a way to afford to stay for two weeks in Dublin, its way too expensive for our meager budget.

She just went on and on telling me of the wonders of Dublin. She was so excited about seeing the sights. I thought I better wait until the last minute to tell her. Okay, so I'm chicken, but a mad Mary is not a nice thing to see.

Finally we each calmed down long enough to watch a movie. Mary was soon sound asleep.

I wished I could sleep. My thoughts kept coming a mile a minute and made no sense.

Why on earth can't I sleep? I'm exhausted, but my brain wouldn't relax. *Wow, air travel is great. But the noise! Heck, I wish I had some earplugs. It would be nice to be able to block out the noise. That poor baby in the row behind me must have an earache.*

I wish I could sleep like Mary. She is also nervous about the flight, but she was snoring away now and I'm a wreck. Oh, well, better check my list:

1. Arrive in London, transfer to an Air Lingus plane, and get to Ireland.
2. Find an ATM, get Irish money. *Will I need English pounds while we're in the airport in London?*
3. Find the car rental service, pick up car.

4. Get map and pray it's in English. *What am I thinking? Of course it will be in English. Do they speak English or Gaelic? God, I hope it's English.*

5. Drive to Mayo! *And don't get killed driving on the wrong side of the road.*

I guess it is a good thing we stop in London to transfer from our United Airlines to our Air Lingus flight to Dublin. It would wake us up a bit before we land in Ireland. I am glad that we will arrive early in the morning. From what I have read, Dublin was a good-sized city and may not be the best place to practice driving on the wrong side of the road.

I wonder what Ireland will be like. It was amazing that we won this trip. Well, not only amazing—it was a bloody miracle. That contest still didn't make sense to me. *Oh, well, I guess I shouldn't question a prize like this.*

---

*"Grandma, what is that a picture of?"* I asked, curious as only a five-year-old could be.

*"Why now, my little angel, if you look close you will see a wee one, even smaller than you were when you were first born. See that one there,"* Grandma said as she pointed to the painting. *"She is the Great Queen herself, the Queen of all the faeries in the world. And there are a great many faeries that is for sure."*

*"But Grandma, why is she crying. Why would a Faerie cry?"*

*"Well, now, the legend is that she had a wee bit of a falling out with a cousin of hers. This cousin was not very nice. She took over the leadership of all the faeries in the land and now instead of spreading good cheer they are*

*forced to cause fear and incite war.  'Tis said that there is only one person in the whole wide world that will be able to help Queen Gráinne regain the crown that is rightfully hers."*

"Can I help her, Grandma? Can I help her find her crown?"

*"Now that is brilliant, Bridget! I think you can help her. Just remember that there are a great many wonders in this land. Sometimes you will hear all the bad things. You must remember to say, 'Be gone now!' and the bad thoughts will go away. Just believe all is possible, and it will be."*

I jerked awake to the sound of a loud snore. I had dozed off. There I sat, trying to look real classy, like I fit in and flew all the time. Now I had drool on my chin, and I think I was snoring. Yup, real classy!

A lady sitting in front of me was talking to her seat mate about a designer she had hired to redesign her bedroom. My thoughts drifted. The places I had lived with Dad had been pretty strange. I had to laugh. I bet no one ever thought of designing those places. *Okay, just don't go there. You will never get yourself back to sleep if you think of the past.*

The mother with the crying baby was humming to calm her. Now that brought back some good memories. When I was little, the people Dad left me with until I was old enough to take care of myself, were so nice. Because of them and their great family, I didn't mind that we lived in a basement.

I remember I called them Grandma and Papa Prendergast. They were superintendents for a large apartment building in the city. Grandma used to tell me some great stories. I wish I could remember some of them. I could listen to her for hours. I could almost hear her saying, in that great Irish brogue, "Be gone with ye now, and don't come back." She would say that to the flies, roaches, or any poor salesman that rang the bell. Soon all of the kids got in the habit of saying it, and that always would make Grandma smile. Now I wonder why I remembered that, maybe I need to say 'worry be gone with ye now and don't come back'. I laughed.

Okay, I'm getting loopy. Gosh, I need to sleep. I can't seem to slow my thoughts enough to settle down. Maybe I should watch a movie. Maybe that would do the trick.

—————————

"Can you believe this line?" Mary grumbled.

I'm way too tired to answer her and just pulled my carry-on another two inches. The room is as large as Grand Central Station. Here we are, finally, in London, and all we can see is the terminal, a few planes, and the runways. How I wish I could see all of London and not just what we could see from the terminal windows. On our way to the baggage claim area we walked slowly past many fantastic shops. It was a nice break.

We stopped at one shop that had some great post-cards. "Hey Mary, look at this one of Big Ben – we should go there someday."

"Look at this, a Ferris wheel right in the city." Mary handed me one that she had been reading. "They call it the London Eye, and you can see all the sights. I would love to see that someday."

We spent some time picking out postcards of places we wished to see. And, of course, we had to buy something to remind us of England. Mary and I each purchased a large cylinder-shaped tin filled with cookies. We thought they would be fun to keep as cookie canisters and wouldn't break while we were traveling around. Mary's tin had pictures of the Queen, King, and

Buckingham Palace. My tin had pictures of Big Ben, the Tower, and London Bridge.

I couldn't understand all that the salesgirl said about the rate of exchange, but she was very nice. She was even able to take our American money and give us change. We didn't want to carry another thing, so I just jammed both of the cookie tins into my satchel.

After getting our luggage, we entered this giant room of lines. There had to be a thousand people from all over the world waiting to go through customs. Everyone stood in what looked like thirty lines, all separated by rope dividers.

Finally it was our turn. We placed our bags on the scanner to be X-rayed, and I walked under the metal detector. I looked back at Mary who was still grumbling about having to take off her shoes.

A man in a uniform asked me if the bright red bag belonged to me. I smiled at this great-looking guy. *God, I love hearing that English accent.* "Yes, but that's not just any bag. that's a Coach Hobo satchel. It was such a steal."

He wasn't smiling back, so I thought maybe he doesn't understand English. "Ah, I mean *on sale*, isn't it great? I didn't mean to imply that I stole it, just that I got it for a great price, you know what I mean? It's a satchel, large enough to hold all of the last minute things I forgot to pack in my suitcases."

I was still smiling and trying to make this guy, who looked like he was from India, understand me. The next thing I knew, I was surrounded by six cops—or I should say Bobbies--and asked to "please come along."

"What is wrong?" I asked. "Is it too large? Did I pack too much? Is it too heavy?" None of my questions were answered, and I was moved to an area off to the side, away from the flow of traffic. I called out to Mary, as I noticed her looking around for me.

"Is that your friend?" one very fine-looking young officer asked.

"Yes, she is," I answered, and he nodded at two more guys in suits and they were soon on both sides of Mary.

"Please tell me what this is all about," I pleaded. "I didn't steal that bag that's just a figure of speech. You know, like hey, such a deal. You know what I mean?"

An older customs officer asked me to take a look at the monitor. They had my bag on a table. I had been escorted over to the side area so quickly I had not even noticed what they did with my bag. I looked at the monitor.

"Was there any time that you left your bag unattended?" he asked.

"No, of course not! Hey, I'm from Brooklyn, and I know how to take care of my stuff." I was trying to stay cool since I'm a foreigner, but I was beginning to get ticked.

"Is there anything in the bag miss, which does not belong to you?" the officer asked.

"Well, from what I can see on the monitor, it all looks okay to me."

They looked at each other, and Officer Hottie responded.

"Please open your bag, miss, and remove your items, if you will."

"Sure I will, but I still don't know what the problem is," I nervously answered. I removed my spare underwear (according to Mary's mom, you never knew when the airlines may lose your bag), the latest Stephanie Myers  novel, guide books, tickets, and dozens of notes I made to remind me of things that I needed to do before we left.

When I removed my curling iron with its long cord, a couple of the men stepped back. I also removed the two large tins of recently purchased cookies.

I'm so nervous I keep rambling. "What did I do wrong, or is this a normal security measure?" I asked again. And again, I received no answer, just more questions.

I answered their questions, showed my license and ticket, and emptied my wallet and purse. When it looked like they were finally coming to an end, I looked over to Mary, and it looked like she was also being questioned. I could see one of the giants, who towered over her, taking notes.

I continued to pull tissues, devil dogs, pens, etcetera from my bag. Then, with what sounded like a long release of breath, the senior customs officer asked, "I noticed the seal on these tins, miss. May I see your receipt?"

I reached into my jacket pocket and handed him the receipt. For the first time, he smiled and said, "We only have a few more questions for you, if you don't mind."

After I gave him the address of our final destination in Ireland, Officer Hottie, or Charlie Boyle, Senior Security Agent (as his name tag read) said, "Would you like to see what caused the fuss, miss?" Mary had joined me and we both answered at the same time, "You bet."

Charlie pointed again to the monitor and showed us a picture they had saved. It looked the same to me. I could see my paperback, the tins of cookies and…

"*Oh, my Gawd!*" Mary shouted, pointing at the monitor. Then I saw it. The cord from the curling iron had wrapped itself around the two tins, and on the monitor they looked just like two home-made bombs.

"Sorry for the trouble, miss, but we cannot be too careful these days. Please give me a call anytime, and let me know if I can ever be of service," Agent Boyle said, handing me his business card, which I didn't even look at. All I could see was his beautiful smile.

Now that I was really looking at him, boy is he good looking. He is wearing a cap, but I can see that his hair is wavy and a light brown color that goes well with his sky-blue eyes. He is over six feet tall and around two hundred pounds, without an ounce of fat on his sturdy frame.

Wow, Charlie is built. He looks as if he works out in a gym on a regular basis. I looked at his card and again at him and smiled. With his movie-star good looks and athletic build, he looks like a lead in a pirate saga. "Thank you, Mr. Boyle. No problem."

Mary and I laughed in pure embarrassment as we walked away. I told her that we were so lucky we were not in New York. There, I think we would've been spread-eagle on the floor with our hands behind our heads as we waited for the bomb squad. Here we got to meet a hunk and get his business card.

"Well, Miss Bridget," she said. "Welcome to England."

## Chapter 2
# Welcome To Ireland

"I can't believe we're really here," I said to Mary for the tenth time since picking up our luggage at the small Dublin Airport. It didn't feel like we were in a foreign country until I got my Euro's out of the ATM. We paid for the car and were now walking around the parking lot to try to find it.

"There it is!" Mary said pointing to a car 'bout the size of a Volkswagen bug.

"The write up on line said that the Fiat would hold four people and two pieces of luggage, how is that possible? Do we have to put the luggage on the top rack?"

"No Bridge, we can do it, just look for a shoe horn," she laughed.

*I love the sound of laughter; we use to laugh a lot when Mary's Mom was alive.*

"Now I understand what they meant by a three door car. They counted the hatchback." I lifted the door and was amazed at the amount of room for our luggage. It will be a tight squeeze, but I think your right, it will all fit."

After getting in the passenger side first, we finally got our bearings. I practiced driving five miles per hour, on the wrong side of the road, around the parking lot, while Mary shut her eyes and said every prayer she could remember. When I felt a little more relaxed and familiar with how the car operated, I ventured out into the traffic. We found the main highway going west and thank goodness the traffic was light. It wasn't long before we were out of the city of Dublin and heading for Mayo. I explained my reasons for leaving Dublin to Mary and she didn't say anything although I could see she was disappointed.

When we left the main highway we made a couple or wrong turns but the people were very helpful and our main problem was cutting the conversation short to keep going. After this happened the third time Mary said, "Now I know why people love this country, they *like Americans* here. That's cool."

"I know the people here really make this a nice place to be."

---

"I can't believe it took us only four hours to drive across the whole country. It's still early, what do you think of dropping off our luggage at the B&B then going to meet the lawyer and get it over with?"

"Sure let's go, I know you have been dying to meet Maureen and I'm anxious to check out where we will be sleeping," Mary agreed.

We drove to a town called Killkeary, and followed the directions I had printed off from the website to find 'Hillcrest'.

"Wow, I wasn't expecting this," Mary said, and we parked the car in front of a modern looking ranch style home. We knocked on the door and were greeted by the owner. She introduced herself as Barbara Carney and showed us to a formal dining room set up with an entrance from the living room and one from the kitchen. The dining room was ready for the morning: each of the six small tables held four beautiful place settings, each with its own teapot.

Barbara invited us to sit at one of the tables, served us some great-tasting hot tea and gave us a plate of homemade cookies.

"Now what are two young girls doing on their own in the west of Ireland?" she asked.

"My father was from the next town over and I inherited the farm when my uncle passed away." When I told her where it was located and what my mother's maiden name was, she smiled and let me know that she was a cousin of mine, on my mother's side. I was shocked. I knew that I was coming to my father's home, but I had totally forgotten that my mother's family was in this area also. After tea, we put the luggage in our room and drove to Ballina.

A few miles from our B&B, we arrived in my father's birthplace; I pulled over and just looked at the streets that my dad walked as a child.

"Hey this looks like a picture postcard." Mary said as she looked around. "What is the lawyer's address?"

"All I have is Main Street; do you see any street signs?"

We drove from the top of the village with its beautiful ancient church the size of a Cathedral you would find in a much larger city, down one street that ended at a 'T'. We took a left and the business section of the town ended in one very short block. We turned around and took the right section of the 'T' and it also ended in one short block, still no street names.

"Well I guess we get out and walk."

I parked the car at the bottom of what we took as Main Street and walked back up towards the church. The town was made up of two and three story brick buildings, built right next to each other with no spaces in-between. A few had the aged natural brick color but most were painted a bright color. We saw yellow with red around the windows and blue painted brick with white trim, green with red and even a blue gray with pink trim.

"Just looking at this town makes you want to smile, doesn't it?" I asked Mary but she was busy looking in the store windows. The businesses were on the first floor with large glass windows showing the displays, and it looked like there were apartments on the upper levels.

We headed for a dark brick building with an ancient old wooden door. The only thing making it different from all of the other buildings was that it had no storefront window and it had a discrete gold plated sign that informed us that we've arrived at the solicitors' office.

I opened the door and was greeted by the dark. The entrance was dimly lit by an antique yellow glass lamp leading towards a long narrow hallway with dark wood paneling and worn wooden floors. The oppressive darkness was broken only by the bright color of a brochure of white and green on a wood desk set against the wall. We closed the door behind us and were headed for a flight of stairs at the end of the hall when we were struck by a shaft of light as a portion of the wall opened. Mary yelped and we were both ready to run until we realized we were looking at a Dutch door with only the top portion open.

"May I help you?" asked a girl our age, around nineteen or twenty, but dressed in grandma attire she looked older, in a heavy, black wool suit with a white blouse buttoned to her neck. Her only jewelry was a discrete gold chain showing just a little between the collar points. Not a designer I recognized, by the looks of it, it might even be homemade. Not badly made, but sort of depressing looking.

"My name is Bridget Carin, is Maureen O'Hara available?"

"One moment, please have a seat and someone will see to you right off." She pointed down the hall to what I guessed was the waiting room.

We both took a seat but the chairs must have been made to make sure you didn't hang around very long. The chairs matched the desk, either black wood or just black with age and not very comfortable. After ten minutes we were getting ready to leave when a woman, a little older than the first, maybe twenty-five came up to us.

"Are you Miss Carin?"

"Yes, and this is my friend Mary Gallagher." She turned her heavy black rimmed glass covered eyes in Mary's direction and asked, "Are you related to the Gallagher's in Ballina?"

"No, I..." Mary began to answer but was interrupted as this person turned to me and said, "I am Miss Horkan, here is my card. I am your legal representative. Ms. O'Hara is no longer employed by the firm. "If you care to speak with me you really should call for an appointment, we are very busy."

I took her card and said, "Thanks, I'll be in touch," and left before Mary or I showed some Brooklyn attitude.

As soon as we got to the car Mary said, "Well that was a waste of time, where to now?"

"I'm beat, let's grab a bite to eat at that restaurant over there and drive back to the B&B and call it an early night. We can check out the land I inherited in the morning."

The next morning we drove to the land and parked in front of what was my family home.

"We came over three thousand miles to look at a shack for cows," Mary said.

"You have to look beyond the house, Mary. This is, well, I'm not sure what this is. Not far from the town of Ballina, a section of land called Garnaqugoue. Even the name sounds special, doesn't it? This is where my father was born and his father, and back as far as recorded time, the Carin family has lived."

"Well now it's a home for cows and depressing."

I knew that Mary was upset because a farm is not her picture of Ireland and she was still ticked off at the welcome we received from my new lawyer. She would much rather be in Dublin seeing the historical sites. I just had this strong gut feeling. I had to come to Garnaqugoue right away.

I looked at my family's cottage. I could imagine it with white-washed stone walls, the smoke trailing up from the chimney, and—

"Yikes! Did you see that?" I yelped.

"No!" Mary said, with her hands wrapped around her body. "How can you expect anyone to see anything in this rain? I'm going back to the car," she said, as she stomped through the mud to the little rental car waiting in the drive.

*I swear I saw something run over my feet.* It looked small and green. But I didn't think it was a bug. It was too big for a bug and too small for a rat. Oh, well, this is the country. It could be anything.

I looked out over the green hills and couldn't help but smile. I could feel the soft rain on my face as I inhaled the fresh tang of springtime. The sweet fragrance of new leaves, freshly mowed fields and the heavenly scent of blossoms were unfortunately spoiled by the strong scent of manure coming from my family home.

Wow! I'm in Ireland! I can't believe that I'm finally here. It's so unlike anything I've ever seen. There are a dozen shades of green, and it's so peaceful.

Heck, we hadn't seen a soul since we turned on to the dirt road a few miles back. No cars and no people, just sheep and cows. The silence is unbelievable. Without the noise of cars, sirens, and people talking, I can even hear the birds sing.

Breaking this absolute silence was Mary, still grumbling and complaining. I guessed we should have stayed a night or so in Dublin so she could see the sites before I took off for the country. Oh, well, I knew from past experience that it was too hard to explain my feelings to Mary; she would never understand the strong urge I had to come here right away.

I tried to ignore Mary's comments. As I turned to speak with her, I watched her trying to get into the car we rented, with her book bag still on her back. I had to smile at my dear friend. I decided to let her be on her own for a while, as that suited my plans as well. I turned back to look at what used to be my family home, vacant now for over twelve years.

The guide books showed us what Irish cottages looked like, so when I looked at the red tin roof, I could picture beautiful, golden thatch. The walls of fieldstone that should have been white were now gray and black.

*What is that black stuff—mold and moss? Yuck!* All those books I'd read with romantic old cottages neglected to mention mold.

I took a few steps along the path to a large area about the size of a patio. Surrounded with what looks like barbed wire. It could've been for pigs at one time, I guess. I'm not sure, because now it looks like a dump area. I would've liked to see this place when my dad was a boy, playing in the field with his brothers. Of course his sister would've been helping her mom in the house. It's wonderful that my Uncle stayed behind to care for the family farm. I wonder what he was like. I still can't believe this land and home belongs to me, it doesn't feel right. Something about this is making my skin crawl, but what?

Maureen, the lawyer who wrote to me about the death of my uncle, was a great help. She told me about a neighbor who had cleared out my family home and was now using the land to graze his cattle. I called him a trespasser, but Maureen referred to him as a tenant. *"Yeah, a tenant who is not paying rent,"* I grumbled.

I guess anything he decided wasn't valuable he must have thrown into that pile. The rain and time had taken away any chance that I might recognize the precious family possessions they might once have been.

I walked up the beaten path and placed my hand on the old front door. It was made of wooden slats and the top opened separately from the bottom part. *Hah! It's funny that the tenant didn't take this door. He took everything else of value. This door would sell for a couple hundred at home.*

Mary's Mom's favorite pastime was going to garage sales and antique shops, and she would drag us both along with her. Now Mary was into watching the home decorating channel so I know that these doors are in demand. I had to smile at the picture that flashed in my mind of me trying to get the door on the plane. *Darn, this would be an antique that meant something to me.* The wood had retained some of the original bright emerald green paint. I loved it.

No, it isn't only the door. I want the home and the land. I

could picture it with fresh whitewash and flowers. It would look grand, as they say over here. Yup, really grand!

I felt a little hesitation about entering the cottage. I knew that the tenant lived around here somewhere. When Maureen sent me directions to find my old family farm, she told me that the tenant is using the house as a barn for his cows. But seeing it destroyed like this was hard.

I turned once more to look over the landscape that I had loved at first sight, to gather my courage to go inside. I noticed the cows in the pasture, but thank God the tenant is nowhere around, I'm not ready to speak with him. I guess I'd better get over this queasiness and take a quick peek inside before he shows up.

As I pulled open the door, I felt an overwhelming sense of sadness. It was very hard to take a single step into the cottage. The scene that greeted me was a dark room with a large fireplace taking up one whole wall. There is one small room behind the main room and an even smaller room to the right.

It was hard to imagine that this was once a home that housed six people. The rough slate floors were covered with manure. The old straw and the odor added to my feeling of despair. I couldn't stay. All that was my families was gone now, anyway.

As I turned to leave, I noticed something white on the floor. I reached down, and there, peeking up from the straw and muck was an old photo. I cleaned it off the best I could with some Kleenex. *Am I looking at a black-and-white photo of myself?*

I brought it closer to the door to get some more light. No, it wasn't my picture. I was looking at a woman around thirty years of age standing outside a beautiful white cottage with fresh white paint and a freshly thatched roof. There were planters filled to the brim with a variety of flowers, and the woman stood in the sunshine with a smile that would light up the darkest day.

Her hair was dark. She wore a simple cotton dress, circa 1980. She didn't look very tall, maybe around my height of five feet five.

I wished the tenant at least had had the respect to save the pictures, but I had heard from Maureen that he was very nasty and not to expect much from him. This picture was a family heirloom, and to someone like me, who had been alone for so long, it was so hard to explain how much it meant. I never knew my mother but she exists for me through others. Whenever we met someone from our past, which wasn't often, they would tell me stories of how wonderful and kind she was. "She never knew a stranger" was one of the favorite stories of her. I had to ask dad what that meant and for once he actually answered me. "Your mother was a saint. She would know if someone needed to talk and she would always be there for them with a kind word or a shoulder to cry on."

I was holding a picture of my mother. Grandma Prendergast had one of her but I didn't remember it until just now. Maybe this one was taken when she made a visit back home to Ireland to visit family. It must have been after she married my dad, since this was his home. Maybe she knew them before; no I remember Grandma said that they met in New York at an Irish dance. Maybe it was their honeymoon trip, she looks so happy. Yeah, it would have to be the honeymoon, from what I heard she was very seldom happy much after that.

Standing there in the dark, sad cottage, I started to remember more of the stories that I was told. They said that my mother was loved by all that knew her and people were sorry that she died at my birth. I heard the horror of my birth many times. I was the tenth child. All the others had died at birth or a few days later. I was born on October tenth, weighing two pounds, three ounces.

The hospital had released my mother from her bed on October twentieth. As she carried me down the steps, she handed me to my father and asked him to watch over me. Seconds later she was dead.

If she only knew how much my father would blame me for killing her, she never would've left. I cried for the mother I had lost and the pain my father had suffered. Something I had never been able to do, must be the Irish air.

I heard the obnoxious sound of a horn and an angry shout from Mary. "Hey, what's the matter with you? Did you die in there? Come on, get a move on. I'm dying here."

## Chapter 3

# Mystery land

I returned to the car, slid behind the wheel and thank goodness it started right away. I definitely didn't want to have the car break down here and have to wait to get help from the tenant. I made a U-turn in the small area in front of the barn.

The barn, like the house, had flat stones set one upon the other with only an opening for a door and two windows. No attempt had been made to whitewash the barn. The natural stone had fared much better with the passing of time. The barn showed no sign of moss and mold . . . but any farmer in the States would've been surprised at the term *barn*, since it was only the size of a one-car garage. It had served the purpose for my family. This barn probably just housed the hay and one cow for milking.

I slowly drove down the tree-lined lane that was the driveway leading to the house. It was about three city blocks long, and was the prettiest sight I had ever seen. The light rain added a brilliant shine to the green of the hills and trees.

At the bed-and-breakfast that morning, they called it a 'soft day'. It wasn't a hard rain like those that cleaned the streets in

Brooklyn, but a soft rain, like a gentle mist. It depressed Mary, but nothing in this country could ever depress me for long. I felt so emotional. It wasn't like me to cry very often but with these feelings I also had a strong sense of peace.

I pulled out of the driveway and turned left onto a single-lane dirt road toward Knock Airport. There were no wooden fences in most of Ireland, for trees were scarce. Instead, there were many fences of stone that somehow looked just right with all the stone cottages.

There were several homes falling into disrepair across the road from my land. It was a sad sight to see, one that you see much too often in Ireland. Families had to leave their homes to survive. They traveled all over the world to find work and support those left behind.

My father had worked his way over to New York. If not for his brother who stayed on the farm, I guess my land would look just as deserted as these other houses after my uncle died. So the tenant helped a little, in that respect.

I knew from the map the lawyer had mailed that there was a strip of land that separated the family homestead into two blocks of land. The family land consisted of twenty acres, or what they call hectares, on each side of this narrow piece of land. No matter how much research we did, we couldn't find out who owned this property. It wasn't claimed by any owner, and we wondered why. We drove for only a few minutes, and then turned left onto the strip of land that Mary and I had started calling "the mystery land." It was the width of a very narrow one-lane highway. I noticed that the dirt road, with its rocks and grass, showed no signs of any car, cart, or livestock ever traveling upon it.

I don't know why, but I knew that I had to travel the road to the end, which wasn't far since the whole lane was only about five city blocks long. I parked the car beside a large mound of earth that was completely covered with small, blue-gray stones. They were unlike the millions of larger gray stones that were used to build fences and cottages.

Each stone on the mound was round and about the size that would fit in the palm of your hand. The mound was about thirty feet long, six feet tall, and ten feet wide. It might have been my imagination, but it looked like each of those stones contained crystals. The mound seemed to give out a glow that brightened everything around it, even on this gray day.

"Oh, my Gawd, this is an ancient burial mound!" yelled Mary. "Hey, Bridget, how did you know this was here? Like, it's real and I get to see it. Oh, my Gawd! It's not even on my map and not in any of the books, not even my travel guide. I don't even see a marker. Do you think this is . . ." Mary continued her questions as she ran from the car with her camera.

Mary didn't even pause for breath, and kept on talking. I didn't hear what she said, and she didn't seem to notice that I sat transfixed, looking at the mound. I felt drawn toward it. I slowly left the car without closing the door and began to walk to what I felt was the entrance.

There was no door in the mound or change of appearance in the stones, but somehow I knew that this was the way in. As I came within inches of the mound, I must have tripped, for the next thing I knew, I fell. I put my hand out to cushion my fall, but kept on falling.

I finally landed, not very gracefully, on all fours, on a floor. The floor looked liked something you would see in an ancient temple. The marble was bright and beautiful, a variety of colors, some light blue and some peach. The color wasn't only on the floor but also on the walls. There was no dirt or rocks in sight.

Okay, I thought. If I see a rabbit with a stopwatch, I'm going to scream. As I looked around, I saw a man about five feet tall and thirty years of age, with black, curly hair and beautiful, dark blue eyes. My thoughts began to run a hundred miles a minute and not many of them made sense, which was usually the case when I met with the unexpected. I felt real fear that I was really losing it until I looked into his eyes.

I had read the expression "twinkle in his eyes," but I had never really seen a twinkle. Yup—that was a twinkle all right, like this guy was so happy his eyes were smiling. Uh oh, now the tune of "When Irish Eyes Are Smiling" was going around in my head. *Oh, boy, I'm losing it alright.* What the heck happened?

The next thing I knew, the man let out a loud, musical laugh. It was like the ringing of bells at Christmas. The pure sound of it made me want to smile.

"Now, lass, it seems you like what you see and you still have your wits about you, even though your trip here to visit with us is a wee bit unexpected," he said, the twinkle in his eyes even brighter than before.

"Thank you, I think, but falling is not very unusual for me. I dated a guy once who told me only clumsy people fall. But did I really fall? I mean, I know I'm here. Not that I know where *here* is. But I'm no longer where I was, and here with you must mean that somehow I got here, so I think I must have fallen. Did I? Fall, that is?" I knew I was rambling, but I couldn't seem to stop.

"Well, now, let me introduce myself," he said. "I'm called Padraig and a half dozen other names that would be a wee bit cumbersome to pronounce, so you may call me Padraig."

I stumbled over the name. "Hi, Paw-Ick," I managed to say.

He smiled one of those smiles that say you almost got it right, and he nodded. "It is the old language."

"Oh, you mean Gaelic," I said, rather brilliantly I thought.

He just smiled and nodded in agreement. "And you are Delia Winifred Marie O'Carin," he said.

"Well, Padraig, you have it almost right. My friends call me Bridget; however, those are all of my names, except the O'Carin. My father's last name was Carin."

He smiled, gave a slight little bow, and said, "Ah, now, not to worry. That is one and the same. 'Tis a fine name. Many folks have shortened their names or anglicized them over the years. Then Bridget it is! Welcome, Bridget."

I stood, still a little wobbly, but I couldn't help but try to see the top of his head and behind his back. *Hmm, just hair. Well, I can't see anything poking up.* "Ah, just a little question, if it's okay to ask. Did I hit my head on a rock and are you a . . . uh . . . an . . Irish angel?" I asked hopefully, thinking of all the mischievous things I had done in my life while still anxiously looking to see if Padraig had a set of horns and a tail.

Again I heard the bells of laughter. *Wait, can he hear my thoughts? That wouldn't be good. Someone being able to read my mind wouldn't be good at all. And hey, that's my space, my thoughts. I don't like the idea of anyone else knowing them.*

"Now, Bridget, I'm truly sorry," Padraig said. "I shouldn't be listening to your thoughts. I just wanted to make sure that you were not frightened, for I would like this to be a happy homecoming and to be a wonderful experience for you."

Oh, oh, that did it, homecoming? *Yikes. I must be dead!*

Dead? I'm sorry, but I can't be dead. How is Mary going to

get back to New York? *She will kill me. So what am I thinking? I'm dead. Mary doesn't like to drive on the wrong side of the road. Although she is my best friend, she would tick off these nice, quiet people big time. When she gets upset, they might really think she is crazy.*

Okay, that does it, I will not accept being dead. I'm responsible for Mary, and I have to get her back to New York. In New York she can be crazy, and they understand. Maybe I can get, like, a leave or something, just to take her back.

I knew I was babbling but I couldn't stop myself.... *hey, it's worth asking—*

"Are you the head guy?"

*He doesn't look like the head guy, but that could just be the movies. How would I know? He looks kind of young to be the head guy. He is dressed in a very nice suit, but in green? Would the head guy wear green? Well, in the stories of Ireland the leprechauns wear green.*

"Are you a leprechaun?" I asked before he could answer.

*If there are any leprechauns in New York, I don't think that they would wear green it just doesn't send the right message, not something Donald Trump would wear. Maybe he is the head guy of Ireland?* "Can I talk to the head guy of New York? You know, like, someone that will understand folks from the City. No one outside the City understands the City, although Brooklyn is not really the City but we call it the City . . ."

"Bridget, please compose yourself, you are not dead. You are home in Ireland, where you belong. That is all that I meant to say."

"Geeeze! I could've had a heart attack here. Don't do that to me. Well, where is *here* anyway? Where is Mary? If I can't hear her, then I know she is not here and she will really be upset.

"You see, we grew up together and we depend on each other.

Know what I mean? She is not great at budgeting money but Mary is real smart. She is a research engineer for a computer company that makes games. She works from home and enjoys her two major passions, computers and books. *What the heck am I doing, it sounds like I'm signing her up for a dating service.*

"I know she is really excited about being here, but she really came along on this trip for me. She would really be upset if I just left her like this. What am I doing here?"

"Bridget, you are not dead and Mary is fine. We have waited a long time for you to come and reclaim your home. We have been very worried. You are needed here among your people," he said in that gentle, warm voice.

Okay, that did it. For the second time that day, I cried. I sat down again on that gorgeous, surprisingly warm marble floor and cried myself silly. Years of pain, of being alone with no family, and he said I was home. I put my arms across my chest to hold onto my pain as I had done so often in the past and cried with loud, gulping sobs.

*Padraig must be watching me. Boy, he must really think he is looking at a crazy woman. I have to stop crying.*

As my tears slowed, I felt warm, gentle arms holding me and stroking my hair. I couldn't see for the tears, but Padraig must have been kneeling beside me. *This guy sure smells pretty and has soft hands. Oops, that's not a male chest I'm leaning against. Hmm, are there gay leprechauns?*

I opened my eyes and jumped to my feet. I was looking into a pair of unbelievable dark-green eyes. The woman kneeling before me was stunning. Her hair was an amazing combination of red and gold, and it flowed in waves down her back to below her waist.

Wow, she's beautiful! Someone I would expect to see on an Irish stage. Her face has that regal look, high cheekbones, and clear fragile porcelain skin, with just the slightest tinge of red on her cheeks.

When she stood, she appeared to be about six feet tall. The dress she was wearing was so elegant. It looked like it might be pure silk woven with iridescent blue and green threads in a peacock design. And what looked like real peacock feathers along the neck and long flowing sleeves. The colors were perfect for her and enhanced the green of her eyes. *I can just imagine what she saw when she looked at my tear-stained, blotchy face, yup, no elegant look here.*

"I see a very beautiful soul," she said in a soft, musical voice. "Someone that cares for her friend, and feels the troubles of many, I very much like what I see. I also would like to welcome you home Bridget."

Hearing those kind, loving words, I cried some more. "Ah, okay, so you can hear my thoughts also. What is your name and why am I here?"

"My name is Geraldine, and I am one who has the same blood as your mother, and Padraig here has the same blood as your father."

"Well, that explains a lot. Too bad I had to take after my father. No offense, Padraig. I would've liked to be taller and not so robust, if you know what I mean."

With that ever-present twinkle in his eyes, Padraig just smiled and nodded in the gentle way he had. *He may have the same blood as my father, but gentle is a word I would never associate with my dad.*

"Well, hi, Geraldine," I said, since this lady wasn't someone you would call *Geri*.

Again as if reading my thoughts she said, "Bridget you may

call me Grace for it is a role I played that I most enjoyed."

"Thank you Grace, but where am I and where is Mary?"

"Mary is fine. She is enjoying looking at the mound and re-searching in her books. She is talking, but I don't think she realizes that you are not there to hear her speak. Don't fret yourself; you will be back before she realizes you are gone. As to why you are here, you know a bit of the tale already, isn't that right now? I do believe that your solicitor informed you that a neighbor has been grazing his cattle on your land for the past twelve years and by Irish law is claiming that he now owns it."

"Yes," I said. "Maureen is my lawyer or 'solicitor' as you say over here. I spoke with her a few months ago. She told me that her firm was looking for me all these years and had just recently found where I was living. She was very nice and suggested that I come to Ireland, but there was no way that I could afford the trip.

"I was looking forward to meeting her and was very surprised when I found that she is no longer with the law firm. We drove directly from the airport to Mayo. We first found our bed and breakfast and they told me how to find the law office in the village of Ballina. I went there to meet with her.

"Have you seen their offices?" I rattled on without waiting for an answer. "I felt as if I were in the 1600s. They are great but a little creepy, you know, with those tiny rooms and real dark panel-ing and just about everyone, even girls younger than me, wearing dark colors and all in skirts. It was really something to see.

"I mean, the village is really great. Of course it was a little nerve-racking, because we're not used to driving on the left side of the road. And the streets are so narrow and just about everyone parks wherever they want and the cars are so tiny . . . but the houses are great. The village looks just like the postcards.

"Oh," I said, as I noticed the glazed look in her eyes. "I'm doing it again, just running off at the mouth. I can't seem to help it. It's Ireland. I have not found anything that I don't like. Mary said that I keep saying how beautiful everything is and she is just waiting for me to say, 'Oh, look at that beautiful rat in the ditch.'

When she didn't laugh at my poor attempt at humor, I said, "Oh, right, you were asking about Maureen. They told me at the office that she was no longer with them and assigned me a BA. To me that's a little upsetting. I'm sort of working on my bachelor's degree and it seems like I'm asking advice from a fellow student.

"I really want to go to California and study at JFK University. They have a class there called Transpersonal Counseling. It's the study of the body, mind, and soul. Well, of course they are all connected. You're Irish I don't need to tell you, but . . . Oops, there I go again.

"Anyway, I don't feel very comfortable with the new lawyer. I liked Maureen, and if anyone could've helped me, I know it wouldh've been her."

"Ah, now, how about a cup of tea Bridget?" Grace said, as she put her arm through mine and guided me to another room. "Let us have a cup of tea and we can have a nice talk about what is happening. The young women you met is very competent but cannot help you with what must be done."

I was led to a room that was filled with light from a very large picture window. The walls were painted a color I had never seen before: a combination of orange, gold, and rust. The design in the room, with its beautiful, comfortable furniture, reminded me of the million-dollar homes I had seen on HGTV. The color was soft and warm and everything matched magnificently. The draperies had a large flower print and perfectly set off the matched chairs and sofa. I loved it all. Everything in the room was something that I dreamed of having in a home of my own someday. I immediately felt at ease. It was all very comforting, a dream room.

I was drawn to the large picture window in the far wall. Looking out I could see that we were on a grass-covered hill, spotted here and there by the same beautiful trees that led up the drive to my family's cottage. In the distance, I could see the ocean and hear its soothing sounds. The window was draped in long, flowing draperies that gathered at the floor and had a matching swag across the top.

The sunlight was so warm that you really didn't need a fire, but the fireplace itself was just the thing to add to the comfort. It had tiles surrounding the opening that looked to be hand painted. I wanted just to sit there and enjoy the comfort for hours.

Grace led us toward two overstuffed chairs that were just there to view the fire. An exquisite, hand-carved table was set for two and, of course, the table was covered with a beautiful white Irish lace cloth.

The tea set had to be bisque. It was exquisite bone china, so thin you could see through it. Those delicate teacups were part of a set with a teapot, creamer, sugar bowl, and tray, which must have been over a hundred years old. I had never seen such delicate markings and designs. They were incredible.

As soon as I sat, Grace poured my tea and added my cream and sugar just the way I liked it. Of course, I didn't question how she knew this, just as I didn't question how I could see the ocean or even hear it. Since I walked into my dream room and heard the words 'welcome home' and 'family,' I knew I must have been dreaming, so I thought I would just sit back and enjoy it all.

Grace interrupted my thoughts. "Would you care for a biscuit?" She handed me a plate of cookies you wouldn't see on the shelves at Safeway. I selected a chocolate-covered cookie of angel food filled with orange cream. It melted in my mouth and was delicious.

I was so glad to sit there in comfort and watch the fire. It was so restful and maybe my part in the dream was to think of what was happening. Who were these people, and where was Mary? But right that second, all I could do was moan in pleasure. For the first time in a very long time I felt totally at peace.

"I am so sorry to ask again and disturb your rest, as I can tell that the very mention of this disturbs you, but did the solicitor's office tell you what had happened to Maureen?" Grace asked.

"No, they didn't. I figured she just moved to another job." As I spoke, I looked at Grace and she looked sad. A glazed look came over her eyes. She leaned her head to the side as if she was listening to someone. I looked around, thinking that perhaps Padraig had joined us, but I didn't see anyone.

"Okay, Grace," I said, trying not to sound too pushy. "This is wonderful tea and I needed the rest, but I also need to understand what is going on. The last I looked, there was no ocean in this part of Garnaqugoue. So who are you really and where are we?"

I received a nod of that regal head and a smile. "Aye, you have the Yankee directness. Ah, then, do let us proceed," she said. "First, may I warm up your tea a wee bit?" She proceeded to fill my cup and offered me the cream and sugar this time. She also moved the cookies closer to my side, as if to say, *I think you will need these.*

"I will begin at the beginning. A long time ago we were a happy land, a land where people believed in magic and enjoyed life to the fullest. Then, when the troubles began, faith was lost. Those who retained the faith also retained the use of the gifts we all have but have forgotten to use. In your books and stories, I am called a Faerie, and in Irish folklore Padraig is called a leprechaun."

I just nodded. I had expected as much. Hey, I was in Ireland, right? If this was a dream, I guessed it would all be just perfect as it was. Padraig would look like how I had always pictured a leprechaun to look: short in stature, a little heavy, but a fun-loving character with a great smile. Just like how Bing Crosby looked in those old movies.

Grace looked like a Disney-inspired Queen of all the Faeries, tall and regal. *Am I dreaming, or are they appearing like this to offer me comfort, just as I'm now surrounded by all the earthly things that I love. Okay, I'm now delusional. No way is this for real!*

Grace continued with her tale. "Of course, the leprechauns in your stories are not at all like how they truly are. They are really brilliant," she said, with a warm, glowing smile on her face.

"The stories of faeries also are never close to who we really are. We are like the leprechauns in that we love to help others and try to help make dreams come true whenever possible."

She looked over to me with her beautiful green eyes, as if to see if I understood what she was trying to tell me. She continued in that soft, musical voice. "Most people do not believe in us at all anymore. We provide what is really needed—*not what people think they need.* Today people have a hard time being happy because your TV shows tell them that there are many material things that they must have to be happy, and they don't realize all the wonders that they do have.

Now the leprechauns, they are our eyes and ears. Our soldiers, if need be. They help us any way they can. Unfortunately, they do have a great many things to do, and the world with all its changes is getting to be a much more challenging place these days. They are also limited when it comes to dealing with certain issues, but I will get to that later.

There is the bit about causing mischief. Some do like to do that. Like that little bit about running over your shoes this morning," she said with a bright smile.

Ah ha! *So I really did see and feel something,* I thought, feeling a little saner. "What do you mean, challenging?" I asked. I thought I knew, with the wars and things, but I wanted to hear what a Faerie would think was a challenge.

"Well now, you have a lot on your plate right now. But someday you and I will have another cup of tea and a nice long chat. The gist of our challenge is that people do not listen to us. We come to people as that little voice from within, but have you noticed that most people are never quiet long enough to listen? It is getting very, very difficult to reach people because they think they have no time to just be still."

Be still? What on earth does she mean by that? I thought. *The people I know have work to do; they can't afford to just lie around.*

"'Tis a great shame, you know," she said with a very sad note to her voice. "Life has so much to offer; but when we surround ourselves with such pain, we cannot see the beauty before us. It was that way with your parents. You had the right of it when you looked upon the cottage; it was crowded and full of pain. Your great-grandfather was the first to lose his faith, and the gifts left him as well.

"Your father left his sad home at the early age of twelve and walked to Dublin. There he received a position working on a freighter, shoveling coal. He landed in Canada and worked on a farm in Calgary. His employers promised the world, but mistreated the young men in their care. Your father survived, but he was always a fighter."

I was in shock. This was my dream, so why was I hearing stories about my father? I had heard of how bad it was after my parents got together, the fights and the poverty, so I stopped her storytelling to ask a question.

"If my mother and father knew about these gifts, why were they so poor? Couldn't they just snap their fingers and money would appear?"

"Now, those are not the gifts I am speaking of, but you will learn. In a way, your father was able to use his God-given gift when he survived in Canada. There he may have had hard work, but he was in a beautiful land with the peace of the country and animals around him. That setting put his mind at ease. And in that peace, he was able to think of possible solutions to his hunger and not dwell on the problem of survival."

"In New York, your father was denied work because he had a very limited education. He spent most of his time at the pub with others in a similar situation. Think about that for a while. I know you will understand."

*"I doubt it. I spent many volunteer hours working with victims of abuse and I still don't understand the abusers," I thought.*

She must have noticed the puzzled look on my face and continued explaining. "You see, the more you dwell on a problem and spend time looking at all the material riches that you want, but feel you could never get, the more your mind is filled up with fear. There is no room for anything else. Your father grew very fearful. For some, that fear manifests as anger. With his mind filled with anger, there was no room to listen to solutions. Now, you know that fears have real power. You must never let your fears shape your reality as your father did."

"I am not afraid of anything," I said, but not very convincingly.

"Johnny had dreamed of owning his own pub and making a place for himself in America. He realized that without the ability to read or write there were very few jobs, and the prejudice against immigrants was very strong. Like many, his fear turned to anger. With anger we forget to listen and feel anything but anger. Anger is like a cancer that takes over the body and mind. Where anger is living, nothing else is invited in."

"But he did own a bar, so he did get his dream," I argued. "Why didn't he enjoy it? Why did he have to kill himself drinking?"

"All that knew your mother loved her, and she was brilliant. She was self-taught, only having two years of schooling like your father. She was quiet, sensitive, and loving. Many people came to her with their problems. She helped out at the pub as a bookkeeper and knew solutions would come when they had funds to help others. But your father made her stay away from the pub. He gave away food, and much of the liquor was not being paid for. It made your father feel good to give to others. If she complained that the bills could not be paid, he would fight with her rather than listen. As I said, the fear and anger were there still; it never did leave," continued Grace.

"Okay, I can't take anymore of going down memory lane. Are you saying that part of me is leprechaun from my father's side and I want to fight to help make the world a better place, and I enjoy causing mischief?" I asked, mainly to change the subject from my parents.

"You have a great many gifts, it is not just the gift of mischief that you get from your leprechaun's blood.From your father's side, there are many gifts. For one, you are a strong fighter for what is right. Very little frightens you."

*Not that I show anyway,* I thought.

"From your mother's side, you also have many gifts. One you are familiar with, you are what we know as an Empath, or sensitive. Every individual is endowed with some degree of sensitivity, whether he or she is aware of it. That general sensitivity usually manifests itself in the form of dreams and intuition. Your gift goes beyond that, you are one who feels what another is feeling and, you can, as you would say, read their thoughts."

"No," I objected, but stopped as she raised her hand.

"Please let me continue. I know that you do not want to admit that you have any traits of your father, but he also was a sensitive. He cared deeply for people, and that may be why he was never able to get ahead in a monetary sense. His heart was very giving. Have you never felt the need of another so strongly that it has brought you to tears?"

I let out a sound of surprise that she would know this, but she continued as if she had not heard me.

"If the emotion is strong enough, it can get through the wall of pain and negativity that you have created."

"That would explain my life," I marveled. "Even as I argued with Mary over the impossibility of coming to Ireland, I did feel that I had to come here at all costs. Heck, I even maxed out my credit cards to do it. I just knew I had to. But I don't know how I will be able to help in any way. How I will be able to hire a solicitor to fight for the land or anything like that's beyond me."

"What is needed you already have, so don't look further," Grace said, in her calm, soothing voice that almost made me believe her.

"So what do I have to do? I leave here next week, so I hope that I can do this quickly," I exclaimed.

"Oh, now, Bridget, don't you be limiting yourself by the structure you have placed on your life. Be open and all that you need will come," she said with a smile.

"What do I do?" I asked. "The tenant already has the law of Ireland on his side. Maureen told me it states that if one can show that they have used the land for over twelve years, they can claim that land as theirs. I know it is an ancient law. With the millions of Irish people that had to leave to survive, it left a great deal of land unattended and this gave neighbors an incentive to work a larger area.

"Sure, he is taking over my land, but that's not that big a crime. I had asked Maureen to give it to a cousin or neighbor who could use it. Before she could do that we lost contact. I just knew I had to come over here that something was wrong, but I couldn't afford the trip before we won the contest."

Grace took another drink of her tea. We both enjoyed the silence and companionship of sharing a cup of tea for a few minutes longer, and then she said, "Bridget, I have spoken with Maureen. She would also like to welcome you home."

With that, Grace acted as if she were listening again and said, "Oh" as she looked to the side and laughed. Still laughing her beautiful soft laugh, she turned to me and said, "Maureen especially liked the postcard you sent to her from your holiday out west. It had a cowboy, worse for the drink, and his dog guiding the horse home. You called it Montana's designated driver."

I could feel the blood drain from my face. "Do you, are you, uh . . . ah . . . you're listening to her *right now?*" I asked in a low, squeaky voice. She nodded and smiled.

"Dad used to have long conversations with his sister, who was in heaven, but I thought that was caused by the drink. Since I can't hear or see her, does that mean that she is an, also, ah . . . well, like, a spirit?"

Again, the patient nod, to let me know that she was pleased I understood.

*Dad would say that his sister was "just stopping by for a visit," but since he was usually drunk I never believed him. Grace is not drunk; at least I don't think so.*

"Maureen is dead? How did she die? Oh, dear God, no one really knows what happened, do they? Was she murdered?"

Again a nod, but this time the look on her face was one of deep sadness that even one who was not a sensitive would feel.

"But what can I do? Where do I start? Why haven't the police caught her killer? Do they know who he is?" I asked.

"Well now, it was put about that Maureen ran off with a married man. And since she was a beautiful young woman, no one questioned it."

"But that can't be right," I argued.

"Sure you will need to awaken all of the gifts you have been given in order to help this land and its people, both mortal and immortal, you will face many challenges. First of all you will be working on keeping your land, but keep your eyes and ears open, for you may be able to help find a murderer."

"So you think that her murder has to do with my land?" I asked.

"Well, now," she said. "You have a great deal to think over

and even more to learn in a very short time. Do what you can. We are all very happy that you are home now, and sorry we are that you must face a challenge or two, right away. Yes, a lot is expected of the child of this land."

"But there is no way. It's just not possible," I argued, but it didn't do me any good.

I could tell that she wasn't listening when she said, "You have been chosen as the one to right a great wrong. The final battle will take all of the skills and courage you will remember you possess. But first you will be given small tasks to help you awaken your gifts."

"Please remember that you are never alone. Just listen. Learn to be open and accept all that the world has to offer, and you will succeed. First you must take on the tasks of saving your land and bringing justice."

With those words ringing in my ears, I felt water dripping on my face. My back was so cold. The damp ground was soaking through my fine wool jacket, I began to shake.

Interlude

 "Padraig, I do not understand, why must I assume the form of a dog?"

"Well now, there's that wee problem you have." Instantly, a six-foot, gold framed mirror appeared and Mick looked at his image. A broad-shouldered man with a chiseled face deeply tanned from years of sailing and enjoyment of the outdoors. Laugh lines framed amber colored eyes and his sun-bleached hair curling in waves to his shoulders did nothing to distract from his appearance. Mick laughed at Padraig antics.

"Our Dear Queen has a long memory My Lord. As the handsome Earl of Howth, you are, shall we say attractive to young women; this young lady is our descendent. She wishes for her to concentrate on her lessons.

"This planned meeting is much too soon. From what I have observed Bridget has very scattered thoughts. She will not be strong enough to take in all that must be revealed to her, let alone take on these tasks."

"My Lady," said Padraig, "has waited far too long for what is needed. She cannot be expected to wait much longer."

"I disagree, but if My Lady must move ahead, Bridget will need the protection of my sword. May I have your permission to appear to her in my human form?"

Padraig had to smile at Mick as he tried once again to be released from his task of shape-shifting. "No My Lord, I think her Aunt will be the strength she needs right now. Please go prepare yourself, for your duties will begin shortly. As Mick left Padraig turned to see Grace materialize and smiled. "I think we made an excellent choice My Lady."

*Chapter 4*

# Meet the Family

"Don't you *ever* do that to me again, do you hear me? Never, ever again, you hear?"

I looked up at a very angry and scared Mary. Her blue eyes were red and swollen from tears. I had seen Mary in many emotions, but never this scared.

"Bridget, I was talking to you, and when you didn't answer me, I went looking for you. You were just lying here, and you were so still. You didn't answer, even after I shook you. I thought you had hit your head on a rock and were dead. Don't you *ever, ever* do that *again!*" She cried some more, and even with the rain falling I could see the tears running down her cheeks.

"I'm alright, Mary, please don't worry. Let's go back to the bed-and-breakfast. I think we have had enough sightseeing for today."

With a loud sob Mary helped me to my feet and hugged me very hard.

"Are you sure you're okay? Do you want me to drive?"

"Don't worry. I'm okay," I said. "Do *you* really want to drive in the rain, on the wrong side of the road?" But instead of the smile I was hoping for, I got a sullen pout.

We walked toward the car. I was so amazed that I could talk, and walk, as if nothing had happened. I had said that I was okay to drive to calm Mary down, not because I believed I could even walk.

My mind was spinning with questions. What had just happened? Was it a dream, or reality? I had read a lot of Irish mythology; did all of the stories survive because they were based on truth? Was I not only trying to save my land but also trying to solve a crime?

Hell, I was a Brooklyn girl with no money, and now I was supposed to save my land and solve a murder in a foreign country. Good Grief Charlie Brown, if there was any Irish luck out there I'll need it.

A few miles west of Garnaqugoue, we came to a sign for Kiltimagh. The drive and the wonderful surroundings helped to calm my nerves somewhat. Soon we pulled into the long drive leading to our bed-and-breakfast.

I had noticed how beautiful the home was the night before, a modern, ranch-style building with clean lines. The warm, welcoming light shining through the large oval etched-glass door helped to ease my fears.

We parked in front of the main door and walked into a long hallway, whose lemon-yellow walls gave off a feeling of light and air even on this cloudy, overcast Irish spring day.

The lower portion of the walls had white wainscoting, and the top, with its cheerful paint color, was the perfect backdrop for the large, framed landscapes of Mayo. The hall passed a living room on the left with a turf fire blazing to ward off the chill.

We continued down the hall to our room. What I needed was a cup of tea, and quick. Wow, I thought, I was really coming into this land in a strong way—dying for a good cup of tea instead of a Pepsi.

We stopped at a bright white door. I fished out an old-fashioned skeleton key from my damp fleece pocket and opened the door. When I flicked on the light switch, I admired the room I was too tired to appreciate last night. It was a large, comfortable room containing two full-sized beds.

Mary went over to the heater, which was surrounded by a large metal rack used to keep our bath towels dry. She removed the towels from the rack and hung her jacket on it to dry.

"Mary," I said, with tiredness in my voice. I was hoping to break the strong silence I had endured for the past twenty minutes. "Could you put the towels back on the rack when your coat is dry? I really like the luxury of drying off from a shower with a nice hot towel." She grunted what I accepted as her way of saying okay. During the drive I was too preoccupied with my own thoughts to notice, but now I could see the hurt look in Mary's eyes. She knows that there is something that I'm not telling her. I can't tell her, not yet. I don't even know if it was real.

I walked over to the large built-in wardrobe and picked a sturdy wooden hanger to hang up my coat in the bathroom, hoping not to get the beautiful flower rug wet. The bathroom looked like one you would expect to find in a five-star hotel back home. I hung my coat on the shower rail and washed up.

I didn't want to be alone with my thoughts, but I knew that Mary couldn't answer the questions I had. I let her know that I was going to speak with my cousin Barbara, and left Mary lying on her bed by the window reading her tour books.

At the top of the hallway entrance there was a door to the family portion of the house. I knocked and asked Barbara if she had a second to hear about my day. Barbara's B&B was a wonderful find. While I was calling around for a bed-and-breakfast close to Ballina, I was told to check out Hillcrest.

It has a five-star rating and a list of recommendations from all of its former customers. I couldn't get over the low cost of fifty U.S. dollars a night for the both of us. That cost even included a breakfast fit for a king. My cousin Barbara Carney was a tall woman. In her early fifties, she had curly blond hair cut in a no-nonsense style. She was about my size twelve, but on her it looked great; she stood about four inches taller than my five-foot-five. Barbara looked as if she were a CEO for a Fortune 500 company rather than an owner of a bed-and-breakfast in the country.

Barbara's muscles didn't come from a gym but rather from a long life of hard work. When I first met her, I was struck by her confident business look. She was so much like a Mother Superior I had at St. Teresa's whom I came to love, but only after many years of being frightened of her.

———— ((·)) ————

Barbara welcomed me into her kitchen, and we sat at the family table. This large, bright kitchen, had windows all around that overlooked the green hills and valley. There was a modern, double-sized refrigerator and cupboards on one wall. The stove was like something out of history books and looked somewhat out of place in this modern kitchen. It was twice the size of a normal four-burner stove, and had an extra door on the front for turf.

Mary had done her research, and she had explained to me

what turf was. *"Bridget, it's a little-known fact that peat bogs cover one-sixth of the land of Ireland. That gives the area they cover a treeless brown color, only rarely interrupted by human habitation. Turf is formed when plants, which do not rot in poorly drained land, pile up on one another over the years. The deposits can reach a thickness of thirty feet or more. In places like the Ceide Fields, on the north coast of Mayo, prehistoric houses and stone walls from four thousand years ago have been found."*

In this fantastic bed-and-breakfast, the stove, fireplace, and the heating source of the house burned turf. It smelled great. The kitchen was very welcoming and relaxing. It gave off a sense of family, which I so desperately needed. As we sat and I rather absently took the cup of tea handed to me, I wondered how on earth I was going to mention my conversation with a Faerie.

"Barbara," I started after what seemed like a long period of silence. "I went to see what is left of my father's house today."

She sipped her tea, and gave me a regal nod to continue, just like Grace. She was patient and waited for me to go on.

"I think I found a picture of my mother," I said, and carefully handed her the treasure I had brought with me.

She looked at it and smiled. "Yes, that was taken when she and your father came home for a visit. Your mother knew that my brother Peter was walking about twenty miles a day back and forth to work, and she purchased him a bike. It was a grand bike and he was the first in our family to have one. Oh, how we all loved Delia.

"Now, what is it that is troubling you, Bridget? You left here full of life, yet you return with a look that says you are carrying a hundred pounds of rocks on your shoulders. What happened?"

How on earth was I to tell this strong, brilliant businesswoman that my mother's family was descended from faeries? But wait, she is my mother's family. Wouldn't she know?

"Barbara, I don't know how to ask this," I said meekly while staring into my cup of tea. "What did my mother think of faeries and leprechauns?"

With a startled screech, she jumped up and pushed back her chair. With a pristine, white linen cloth, she began to wipe the already spotless cupboards.

"Well, that is the way of it, is it? I should have known. Well, you won't be hearing any of that old nonsense from me. We are good members of the parish and . . ."

"Please, Barbara, I didn't mean to upset you. I'm just curious, and I need to ask someone. It's not like this is written in any book I have ever read."

"Well, you see," she said, once again taking her seat and lifting her cup. "I never expected you to chat me up about the old ways; it's just not done. No, it's just not done." Then she was silent.

I waited patiently. She finally said, "Well, now, there is always your Aunt Molly."

"Who is Molly?" I asked, very excited to hear that there was someone to speak with.

"Well, now, another of your uncles, on your mother's side that 'tis, met and married a city girl. She sometimes practices the old ways. He left her to find work in England where he lives to this day."

"Wow, another uncle. And he is alive? I don't believe it!" I cried. "Do we have more relatives, besides the uncle in England? How about the one with the bike, is he still alive?"

"Yes, he is very much alive. He has a nice family in the north of England near Blackpool. Bridget, we are a very large family, but you are not to speak with anyone about the wee folk except your Aunt Molly. No other would like to speak of such things."

I left that warm, cozy kitchen after I promised that I wouldn't approach any other person except Aunt Molly. I was given her phone number and found out how I could find her apartment. My aunt lives in Dublin, just a few blocks away from the Guinness brewery.

As I showered and got ready for bed, the day's events kept playing in my head. Aunt Molly shouldn't be too hard to find, and Mary would love to return to Dublin. We had driven on a highway from the airport to the west coast. She never even had a glimpse of the famous landmarks, not even the old library at Trinity College.

The problem would be the cost of a hotel in the city. I had already checked that out and knew it was outrageous and I was running out of euros quickly.

But with Grace's words in my mind, "Be open and all that is needed will come," I fell into a deep, restful sleep and didn't wake to worry about money as I often did back home.

We had a full breakfast of tea, cereal, toast, eggs, sausage, and Irish pudding, or what I knew to be blood sausage. No way on earth was I telling Mary what it really was, for she thought it tasted great.

"Mary, rather than speak with the lawyer and tenant right away, okay if we leave this morning for Dublin?"

Mary was ecstatic "You don't need to ask, I think that's a great idea, why the sudden change of plans?" she asked, looking very suspicious.

"Barbara told me that I have an aunt living in Dublin, and I'm very anxious to meet her."

All through breakfast Mary watched me, silent but curious. I tried not to make eye contact. I'd decided not to tell her about my little encounter, at least not yet. I didn't know how she would take the news that her friend was crazy. Or that she was a mixed breed of a leprechaun and faerie. Knowing Mary, she would either think it was cool or head to the nearest psych ward for help.

We headed to the village of Kiltimagh and the road east to Dublin. It would take us only four hours, but I wanted to leave early enough to find my aunt's home.

Driving for four hours wasn't bad at all. I really enjoyed driving this beautiful countryside. We drove past fields of every possible shade of green with picturesque streams meandering through idyllic valleys. Miles of gray stone walls crisscrossed one another in an ancient pattern. Ireland had it all, including miles of coastline, ancient tombs, monasteries, castles, and possibly leprechauns and faeries.

I enjoyed the peace and quiet so much that not even the noise coming from Mary's headphones bothered me today.

On our hurried drive west to Mayo, we were both too tired to talk much. Mary felt uncomfortable with quiet, and she seemed to always want to fill her head with noise. Today I had way too much to think about to even ask her to turn down her iPod. We stopped for gas at a little station next to a bar called 'Regan's Pub', which looked like a place I would love to check out someday.

I was grateful that Mary didn't want to talk; I had to get my thoughts in order. I really wished that I could talk this all over with her, but not yet. She is so left-brained. She would analyze this all to death and still not believe me.

After an hour of going over my meeting with Grace and Padraig in my head, I decided that maybe I wasn't crazy. I would look into the death of Maureen, hopefully with Molly's help.

Okay, I need a list. I can't help it. It must be something Mary and I both picked up from her mom. I can't function without a list. I have about two hundred euro's left, for both Mary and myself for a week.

The bed-and-breakfast is paid for through the day we fly home, but that will be four hours away from Dublin. Not close enough to spend each night. Although I love the narrow country lanes, I would hate to drive them at night.

1. *No Money.*
2. *No place to stay in Dublin.*
3. *No idea what I'm doing.*
4. *How do I solve a murder?*
5. *How do we eat with no money?*
6. *Why would someone kill over my land?*
7. *What if Aunt Molly turns me away? I'm kind of her step-niece, not someone she would feel obliged to help out.*
8. *No bloody idea what I'm doing.*

# Chapter 5

## Bad Faeire

We drove east, on highway N5 for a couple of hours, and I was ready to stretch my legs. "Mary, wasn't there a historical spot around here that you wanted to see, Sand something-or-other?" I asked.

She removed her headphones and reached for her travel guidebook. "That's right; Sandingham is on the N5, between the town of Rockford and Tulane. I was so tired when we arrived; *since we drove straight through to Mayo,* I forgot to look."

Mary found the right page in her guidebook and began to read. "Sandingham House was built in the 1720s a twenty-thousand-hectare estate with a very impressive family home. Today the estate has been whittled down to a mere one hundred twenty hectares. There is also a famine museum on the property we must see."

"Well, we're almost there. The town of Rockford is just a few more miles," I said, reluctantly. I just remembered an article I read about the famine, which mentioned this place. I was going to tell Mary that this was a sad place to visit, but when I looked over at her she was happily reading her guidebook. *No, I don't have the heart; maybe she will just love all of the history and not be as affected by the sadness as I am.*

We soon came to a beautiful town with very wide streets that led to the arched, grand entrance. The massive twenty-foot black wrought iron gates were open and we could see a large gold leaf embossed on both sides. They were attached to a fence of the same height that looked as if it surrounded the whole one hundred twenty hectares.

"Wow, these guys have money to burn."

We drove along what would equal several city blocks, and all we could see was a park-like setting on both sides of the gravel drive. Large well feed sheep were grazing on the grass. They all had the letter "S" painted in red on their wool, which we thought must have marked them as property of Sandingham in case they wandered off.

The tall old-growth trees were majestic and had to have been there for hundreds of years. There were also younger, flowering trees, and wonderful landscaping that must have included hundreds of different types of flowers. It all was overwhelmingly beautiful.

We came around a curve, and I almost hit the brakes. With the size of the front lawn, I guess I should have been prepared, but nothing could've shocked me more than the size of the mansion in front of me.

"I have seen pictures of Buckingham Palace, and I don't think it's this big. What do you think . . . about two hundred rooms?"

Mary stared at the mansion. "I think impressive is too nice of a word to describe this place. I think *ostentatious* is more like it."

We followed the signs to the side of the main building and

found a parking place. Mary jumped out of her side, her excitement showing with every step she took. I reluctantly turned off the car, removed my seat belt, and reached in the back for my purse. I got out and turned to lock the door, noticing the mess in the backseat. *I really have to clean that up,* I thought, as I followed Mary. I felt as if I was walking in slow motion, my feet dragging with each step.

We entered what looked like a large cafeteria and were directed to the gift shop to buy tickets for the tour.

I was digging in my purse for Euros when Mary came back with a smile on her face and said, "It's only twenty euro's."

"Mary that's more than thirty dollars each, that we don't have."

She lost the smile. "Well, I already bought a ticket so I guess I'm going in."

"Sure, that's okay, I think I will wait in the car for you, and you can tell me all about it."

"Fine with me," she said, turned, and walked down the hall with her ever-present backpack bouncing against her back.

I stopped to look at some of the gifts for sale, but I couldn't find anything I liked that was affordable. I wandered over to the books and began to read a paragraph about the famine . . . and then it hit. I felt dizzy and nauseous. I all but ran toward the parking lot and the safety of the car before I embarrassed myself and got sick on the plastic statues of St. Patrick.

I staggered around and doubled over a few times to hold on to my stomach. I almost made it to the car before my wonderful, full Irish breakfast decided to leave me.

Now I was weak. It took a miracle to find the car key and get the bloody door open. I sat behind the steering wheel and threw my purse on the passenger seat.

I reached into the glove compartment for some tissues and tried to calm myself, but the tears and shakes began. I laid my head back against the headrest and just let it all come. I could see them now, all standing at the gates; their pain and hunger was overwhelming.

Mothers held infants too weak from hunger to cry. Children barely old enough to walk held their mothers skirts. Old folks stood in the cold and damp, looking so frail that if not for the knobby wooden canes holding them up, they would certainly fall. Everything was dark, the clothes, the rain, the clouds, but mostly the blackness of hunger. It was just too much to take in. I laid my head in my hands and cried until there were no more tears, and sobs shook my body.

This type of reaction had hit once before, at a World War II exhibit at the Brooklyn Museum, as I was standing in front of pictures of the holocaust. I guess Grace was right; I'm what the books call an "Empath," someone that picks up on feelings. Usually it's with people who are living, but I guess today it was from people who had left their pain flooding the land I was on.

*"Now, the damn English are at fault for this. We must do something to get even,"* said a bone chilling voice of pure evil. The blood in my veins began to chill. The power of that voice was so strong that I began to shiver in fear. I quickly opened my eyes. There on the dashboard was a *thing* looking at me and I screamed. When I realized that he wasn't coming after me with a knife, just standing on the dashboard of the car and staring, I decided to look him over. I think he's a faerie. He's about five inches tall and dressed in an outfit you would expect to see on Robin Hood: brown leather pants, a white frilly shirt, open down the front, and a cap,

with a long, brown feather sticking out of it and wings. Wings, I have seen them on birds but these were beautiful, translucent wings that left a dusting of gold shimmer whenever they moved. I stared at the small figure, closed and rubbed my eyes.

*"Bejesus! Ye be seeing me?"* he yelped when I finished screaming. This time I heard a softer, much nicer sounding voice.

I took a deep breath, counted to ten, opened my eyes and yup, he's still there. Here we go again, the tourist bureau calls this a magical land, and they are not kidding. "Of course I can see you," I answered. "You're sitting right there, on the dashboard of my car, speaking trash about a whole nation of folks when only one man was *responsible.*"

*"I don't understand you seeing the likes of me, but we can sort that out later. Hey, now lady, cut me some slack, will ye? I am just doing my job."*

I was looking into the saddest eyes I have ever seen. They were beautiful dark obsidian with a touch of amber, but the depth of sadness in them made me want to cry. *"Your job,"* I repeated. "I thought that faeries were happy folks. You don't look like a happy, carefree little faerie. You look as if you ate a whole bag of lemons," I said, trying to understand. This fellow wasn't the happy member of the fae community, I imagined I would meet. Not even as handsome as Darby O'Gill even.

*"Sure now, my job is to remind you just how bad the English people are. Not to be anybody's happy, carefree little faerie,"* he said, and looked even sadder. I could tell that he was getting ready to argue the point with me, and I was just not in the mood.

I looked at him, and said, as Grandma Prendergast would, "Begone with ye now, and don't come back!" The next thing I knew, there was a bright explosion of multi-colored sparkles and the faerie was *gone. Freakin' weird! He looks like a sparkler set off on the Fourth of July. Okay, I'm really losing it; did I just meet a bad Faerie?*

I thought more about what had just happened and decided that it was a daydream brought on by stress. I just couldn't figure out what it was supposed to mean.

I'm worn out. I must have fallen asleep. The next thing I knew, Mary was opening the car door. I expected a bubbly Mary who would tell me about the things she learned for the next fifty miles, but she didn't say a word.

I reached for a wet wipe and washed off my face, hoping to wake up.

"Can I have one of those?" Mary asked as she threw my bag into the back seat and reached over to take a wipe from the pack to wash off her tears.

"How did you like it?" I asked, thinking I might already know. I received no answer to my question. "Wanna stop in this town for lunch?"

"No," she said. "Get us far away from here, please, as soon as you can."

I drove back down the drive, but this time we didn't admire the beauty around us. We were both lost in the pain of the past. Several miles later, Mary asked, "Do you know what happened there?"

"Not all," I said. "But what I know is not good."

In an outraged voice, Mary told me about the potato famine. "People were dying by the thousands. This very rich English lord owned this entire area, but he wouldn't do anything for his tenants.

"About eight hundred people approached his home and begged for food at the gates. He told them that he would do better than food—he would put them on ships to America. The people had to walk over a hundred miles to the port, and many died along the way, but the ones remaining had dreams of prosperity in a new land.

"What they didn't know was that they would be crowded into the cargo hold of ships that were built to hold a third of their number, and that their landlord had not paid for any food or water for them.

"Bridget, they all died at sea. Can you believe that? How could anyone do that? All of the eight hundred men, women and children died!" she cried.

"The tour guide showed us all a twenty-foot painting of the English landlord, and it was so lifelike, just looking at it made me sick. How could someone do that?"

"Mary that's one thing about history: we may never know the full story. Were the English landlord or the ship's captain and crew at fault? We may never know for certain."

We both reached for the tissues and talked for the next couple of hours of the atrocity that man will inflict on another. It's so hard to understand.

*Chapter 6*

# An Unexpected Gift

"Mary, look at that sign for the Genesis Gift Gallery in Mullingar. Do you wanna stop? I need to get a little something for my Aunt Molly. One thing I know for certain about Irish custom is that you never arrive without a little something in hand," I said. *Especially if you need a place to stay and help with your sanity*, I thought.

"Sure," she said. "I would love to see if they have local crafts." We pulled into a drive leading to a large warehouse and gift shop in the middle of what looked like farmland. They were busy; the very businesslike gift shop had a dozen cars parked in front.

"I bet this place has bus tours stop here. Looks like their set up for it," I said, as I entered the beautiful large showroom.

Their specialty is silver, and, boy, how I wished for money to buy some of the beautiful pieces of sculpture. I soon found a nice print made by a local artist for only ten euro and we had it gift wrapped.

This stop was just what we needed to help wash away the misery of our visit to Sandingham. We laughed over some of the souvenirs, and oohed and aahed over the beautiful silver and art works. With this good mood we returned to our car with the goal of finding someplace to eat.

"Why is it whenever you're hungry, you can't find a place to eat?" Mary asked as she searched each road we passed for a fast food place or even a restaurant but found nothing.

The road started getting a little busier with traffic and soon we were back in the suburbs around Dublin. There was a restaurant along the highway that looked like a Howard Johnson's, except it was called "Mother Hubbard." We screeched to a stop, parked, and ran inside. First stop, bathroom and then food.

A tall young man with a mop of bright red hair and amazing smile greeted us at the door. He showed us to seats in the third room of this huge restaurant that was decorated as a country kitchen. A waitress, wearing an old-fashioned uniform, laughed when we told her that we were so hungry we could eat a horse. She soon had us both drinking tea and eating mouth-watering, hot biscuits as the cook worked on our orders.

When we had finished eating and were relaxing over our third cup of tea, I explained to Mary that I hoped we would be able to stay with Aunt Molly, since we were almost out of spending money. Mary was okay with this, but I wondered if Aunt Molly would be. I paid the bill, and Mary headed for the gift shop. I told her that I would meet her in the car.

*Wow, I don't think I should have eaten so much. Now I'm ready for a nap,* I said to myself as I leaned my head back against the headrest.

I heard a whimper. *What the heck is that?* I reached over and checked the radio but it was off. The whimper was louder now. I turned around in my seat to check the back of the car and there it was—a puppy.

He looked to be about a year old. He had the red rust color that the Irish setters have, but it was only around his eyes, ears, and tail. The rest was white with a little curl, except for a few freckly-looking red spots on his face and back.

He just stared at me, and I found myself staring back into the most gorgeous, caring eyes I had ever seen. Deep rich amber colored eyes with a russet/coppery tint, surrounded irises of black obsidian. They say that the eyes are the windows of the soul. If they are right, then I was looking into very ancient eyes. His nose has a reddish cast, and his mouth sagged a little, almost giving him an animated face, which could look like a sneer or a smile. Right now he just looked puzzled.

We would've stayed longer in our staring contest, but Mary opened the door and sat down. The puppy got up, jumped between the seat backs, and landed on Mary's lap.

"*Holy shit*," she yelled and started to push him off, but he whimpered again. She looked into those beautiful amber eyes and was lost.

"Bridget, where on earth did you get a dog?" she asked, as she stroked the silky fur on his back. "Is he a stray? Did some idiot drop him off here with all of this traffic, I hope you got their number, I want those losers shot. This little guy could've been killed." Mary said quietly.

I had to smile, I knew Mary was concerned about the puppy and didn't want to raise her voice to frighten him.

"I didn't get this dog anywhere. I don't know where he came from," I said, when I could get a word in edgewise. "The door was locked . . . and you know I have a habit of checking the backseat before I get in. I tell you Mary, he wasn't there when I got into the car."

I know I should be more freaked out by a dog materializing in our car but hey, I have met a fairy and leprechaun, nothing will surprise me now. I really expected Mary to be freaked out also but I forgot her soft heart, there was no way we could've had an animal in our small apartment, even if the landlord would've allowed it. We both loved animals.

"Maybe he jumped in when you opened the door? Wait a second. What is this on his collar? It looks like paper." Mary tugged at his collar and removed a piece of paper that looked like old parchment. She read: "Please take good care of Mick and return him to Mayo with you when you return. Do you know who this note is from, Bridge? There is no signature." Mary held the paper up for me to take. *I thought I knew who wrote the note. They say that a dog is a great companion, could that be what Grace meant by "remember you are not alone" nah, that can't be what she meant. Could it?*

"Maybe the note is from Barbara, and she wants Aunt Molly to see the dog." *Boy, that made absolutely no sense whatsoever, but I guess Mary didn't give it much thought, because she didn't say anything; she was way too busy playing with the dog. I pulled out into the traffic that kept getting heavier as we approached Dublin.*

"Bridget, what kind of dog do you think this is? I think he looks like a Brittany spaniel, don't you?"

I looked over, and all I could see were those long legs and long . . . "Mary, ah, do you think his, huh, boy parts are supposed to be so big?"

Mary laughed and cooed. "Of course, he is going to be a big boy, now aren't you Mick, me boyo?"

*Okay, great. Now what on earth was I to do with a dog? Grace and Padraig are nuts? I mean, Mary and I love animals, and would love to have a dog, but dear God! That's all I need to do now, worry about a dog. Well, I have to trust that there is a reason for this guy. He is awfully cute.*

We arrived in the city and found the street we were searching for. As we drove around looking for a place to park, we found ourselves looking at the old buildings.

"I don't know about you, but I almost feel like I'm home. The traffic is about the same, but there is something different. Do you know what I mean?" Mary asked.

"Yeah, I know just what you mean. I feel it also. It's funny, like a sense of being home in the old neighborhood, but more relaxed. You have to admit, it's a whole lot cleaner. Do you think it's because we haven't seen any gang graffiti, and we're in a city?"

"That could be it, or maybe it's the wonderful colors. You know, they have the same old brownstones we have, but theirs look more loved."

I laughed and she said, "Cut that out, you know what I mean. Look at the trees and flowers planted on the sidewalks, and all the upbeat, cheery colors on the doors and shutters."

"Hey, look at that one!" Mary pointed to a bright red door with a large, dazzling brass door knocker. Stretching the whole width of the door was an arch of stained glass, with yellow and red flowers. The setting sun must have been hitting it just right, for the rainbow of colors just bounced off the door and lit on many of the cars filled with folks rushing about. It may have been my imagination, but that rainbow of color seemed to slow them down a bit.

We found a place to park. Mary took off her favorite woolen scarf to make a leash and tied it to Mick's collar. She got out on the sidewalk and opened the back door to reach for her suitcase.

"Please leave that for now. We can always come back down to get it if we know for sure we will be staying here," I said. I dragged myself out of the car. I wanted nothing better than a hot shower and a hotter cup of tea; I was bushed.

"Hey, I thought you called your aunt when we stopped for gas," Mary asked.

"I did, but how could I say, hey, I'm your long lost niece and can my friend and I stay with you?"

"No sweat. We will play it by ear," Mary said. "Let's take Mick for a walk before we go up to your aunt's place."

"Great idea," I said, with more enthusiasm than I felt. At this point, I only wanted to get this whole thing over with. Who knows, I thought, maybe Molly will say that there are strange flowers on our land, and the Carin children are allergic to them. And, ha ha, funny thing, they cause all sorts of hallucinations.

*Chapter 7*

# Aunt Molly

Mick took care of business, but when he saw us looking at him, he turned to face us so we didn't see him squat. When he watered every bush and tree we passed, he did it in such a way that the bush, or tree, was between him and our view. Almost as if he was a shy or modest puppy.

As Mary and I watched him, we smiled and I noticed that a change had come over her. The scowling Mary was now transformed into this beautiful, smiling friend, I enjoyed being with. I wondered if it was our stop at Sandingham, the puppy or the trip itself. This *is* the first time she has been on a vacation since her Mom died.

Aunt Molly lived in an apartment complex on the corner. We entered through a wrought iron gate into a courtyard with outside steps leading up to each section. "Her apartment is in this first section, on the sixth floor," I said, as I looked everywhere for an elevator. "Hey, I don't see an elevator, do you?"

"*Nope!* It looks like we're climbing stairs. Want to race?" Mary said, as she and Mick made a beeline for the stairs to race each other to the top.

"You crazy or somethin?" I laughed as their combined six feet went around the first landing before I had a chance to go up even three steps. *Yup, when life calms down, I must lose some more weight and get in shape,* I told myself as I climbed my way up to the sixth floor landing, trying not to look ancient by holding onto the railing with both hands.

Mary and Mick were stopped in front of apartment two. "Well, here we go," I said, and used the brass door knocker to knock on the brilliantly painted blue door. Within seconds a woman opened the door. She was shorter than me and had a wonderful smile that was contagious.

"Oh, now, you must be Bridget," she said, looking directly at me, although Mary was in front of her. Turning to Mary, she said, "And you are her good friend Mary. Welcome, please come in."

"Ah, bejesus, what do we have here?" she asked, noticing Mick. She crouched down to his level and put out her hand. "And who may you be, my good man?" she asked, looking Mick in the eye and putting out her hand as if to shake hands with a human.

"Oh, my Gawd, look at that would ya? He shook her hand. See, I told you Mick was one smart puppy," Mary said, sounding very much like a proud Mother when her child did well, as she and I watched Molly and Mick getting acquainted.

Molly and the dog were having that staring contest he and I had, but something told me that Molly was doing more than just looking into his eyes. *What, like checking to see if he is house trained? Dear God, I didn't think of that! I sure hope he is.*

Aunt Molly stood up and led us all into the hallway. She opened the first door on the right and showed us a beautiful large bedroom with two twin beds. "Now, this is where you both will be staying. Across the way is the bath, with all you may be needing."

*We can stay here! She didn't even expect us to stay someplace else. That's so wonderful. Oh, my God, I feel like I'm tearing up again. This is so great!*

She continued down the hall, passing another door I took to be her bedroom, and led us into a very large living room. The first thing I noticed were the two tall windows that reached almost to the ceiling. Each had a window seat with wonderful cushions that looked as if they were covered in some ancient fabric that looked like hand woven tapestry. I found myself daydreaming of curling up on one of those cushions with a good book and a hot cup of tea.

"Now then, you must be starved. Why don't we have some tea," Aunt Molly said, as she hurried toward a kitchen the size of a small bathroom. "Sit yourselves down," she said, pointing to the two overstuffed couches with a large round coffee table in front of them that must also serve as a kitchen table.

"Can I help you, Aunt Molly?" I asked, walking toward the kitchen.

"Now, don't you worry yourself, we are all set," she said, as she walked towards me with a large serving tray filled to the brim with sandwiches, buns of every kind, a teapot, cups, and even something that looked like a saucer of chopped liver for Mick.

"Boy, that was fast," I said, as I sat down on the couch before I fell down. Mary turned from checking out the bookshelves and gasped at the amount of food.

"Oh, now, it is just a little something to tide you over for a bit," she said, as she placed the tray, that looked way too large for her to carry, on the coffee table.

She then set down the plate of liver for Mick and told him to finish it before he had a bun. Molly poured out our tea and handed us plates piled high with a variety of sandwiches and cakes. She then took a small soup bowl, added tea, with cream and sugar, stirred it up, and set it down for Mick.

I was going to protest that dogs only drank water, but Mick looked at me and quickly finished all of the tea Molly had poured for him. The whole time this was going on Molly was talking in a voice I can only describe as excited. Yup, that was it, she sounded excited that we were there and just excited with life. I loved her right away.

Here was a woman living on her own, over fifty years of age, and she glowed with life and laughter. Here was someone I could talk to. Someone who wouldn't think I was crazy, *I hope.*

"Now girls, eat up, please don't be shy, there is plenty more where that comes from," Molly encouraged.

I was going to tell her that we just ate a few hours ago but I noticed that both Mary and I had enjoyed the food and there was very little left on our plates.

Molly told us of the family and of her neighbors. She asked many questions about New York but never asked us about our families. When we were all done, Molly rose to gather the empty plates.

"Please let us help you with those Aunt Molly."

"I wouldn't think of it, and didn't you just drive all the way across Ireland today? You must both be tired. I will wash up and then we can have a nice chat."

Mary and I tried again and insisted she sit and rest while we cleaned up the dishes, but she wouldh've nothing to do with our suggestion.

"None of that, you are family and guests in my home. Sit there and relax." Molly informed us, in a tone of voice reminiscent of the nuns that taught us both. It was a tone that booked no argument.

I couldn't sit and watch her work. "Mary," I said, "Why don't we walk Mick and get our suitcases?"

"Great idea," she said. "I think he will need to take care of business, since he drank three bowls of tea and ate two muffins . . . plus all that liver."

Molly laughed at the look of embarrassment on Mick's face and headed toward the kitchen.

We walked down the stairs at a more leisurely pace, full as we were with pounds of wonderful food and hot tea. Mick pulled Mary along as we neared the street and headed right for a tree; we laughed and smiled at his antics. We retrieved the two suitcases and camera from the trunk and headed back.

"What do you think of Aunt Molly?"

"I love her; do you think it would be okay if I called her Aunt Molly also?" Mary asked.

"Of course," I said. "I think she would like that."

"Mary, does Aunt Molly remind you of someone?"

We both looked at each other and then said at the same time "Mrs. Slotnick!" and burst out laughing.

"It's not only her intelligent blue eyes and blonde hair, even her chutzpah is the same, Ai-Vay" Mary laughed. "Who would think Mrs. Slotnick from Israel would have a twin in Dublin."

"Remember how your mother and Mrs. Slotnick loved watching those old murder mysteries? They even had us hooked. We loved to uncover who the villain was before the end of the show," I laughed remembering. *But there is something else, I thought.*

*She certainly has that look of intelligence a crime solving detective would need, but to get that meal to us so quickly, I wonder if she has a little touch of the magic herself.*

When we let ourselves into the apartment and put the suitcases on the beds, Mary said, "You know, I think I will take a hot shower, crawl into bed, and read. Would that be okay, not antisocial or anything?"

I was glad I was near the bed, because I sat down abruptly. *Okay, now this is a major change.* Mary never minded what people thought of her, and she always did whatever she wanted.

"No," I choked out. "I really think that's a great idea. We're both really bushed from the drive."

A shower seemed like a great idea to me also, but what I really needed to do right away was to speak privately with Aunt Molly—and the sooner the better.

I went into the living room to find Mick sitting on the couch, next to Molly.

"Bad dog!" I yelled. "Get down off the furniture." Mick looked as if he would ignore me, but Molly placed her hand on his rump and he took one look at her and jumped down.

"Aunt Molly, do you have a second? There is so much I would love to speak with you about."

"Of course, sit here beside me so we can have a nice private chat," Molly said patting the sofa.

*Hmm, private chat? Now why had she said that? How did she know that I needed a private chat? Oh well, that was what I wanted.*

"Mary is in the shower, and then she plans on going to bed to read up on all of the sites she wants to visit tomorrow. She hopes that's okay."

"Well, of course, and why wouldn't it be? She is a guest in

my home, and has every right to be as comfortable as possible," Molly said. "And it may be that your friend knows you have a lot on your mind and would like to speak with me."

"A few days ago I would've said that you were wrong . . . but something has come over Mary within the past few hours. She might be thinking of what I need, rather than her own comfort. No, that couldn't be it. Not Mary. She couldn't have changed that much, that fast, could she?" I asked.

"Well, now, I do not know Mary, but I will ask you this— when did the change come over her. Or should I say, when did you notice the change come over her?"

"I was asking myself just the same thing," I said. "Could it have been the pain of visiting Sandingham, or the wonder of holding and playing with a puppy like Mick? Something did it, and I'm not complaining, mind you.

Aunt Molly smiled. "Now maybe she was meant to be a partner in your adventure."

I looked at Molly. She couldn't have known what had taken place in Mayo. Or could she? What did she mean? *Oh, I'm imagining things; maybe she just means my adventure of coming to Ireland.*

"Well, that's just it; I'm having a strange visit . . ." and just as I was going to go into detail, the shower stopped. I didn't hear it stop, but I noticed that Mick had gone to stand by the bathroom door as if waiting for Mary to appear. And she did.

Aunt Molly called out to her "Did you find all that you needed, Mary?"

"Oh, yes," Mary said, coming into the living room with a towel wrapped around her head, Indian-style. "It felt great; I'm so relaxed now. I was thinking of lying down to read, if that's okay?"

"Of course it is, I know you will want to get an early start seeing the sights. Be off with you, now, and have a good rest. I will have a grand breakfast for you in the morning," Aunt Molly said, as she went over to Mary to give her a hug. I could see Mary's eyes and I knew that that hug meant a great deal to her.

The bedroom door closed, and Aunt Molly suggested we have a nice cup of tea with our chat. We both went into the kitchen to gather the tea things. She had one of those electric teapots that boiled water very fast, and by the time I added the tea bags to the pot, gathered up the milk and sugar, it was ready to pour.

*Boy, I have to find one of these electric teapots as soon as I get home—they are great.*

Soon I was again sitting on the couch, eating biscuits and drinking tea. I had to admit that a nice, hot cup of tea sure had a way of helping me relax. Well, at least somewhat.

"Now why don't you go ahead and tell me about your trip to Mayo?" Aunt Molly asked, as she settled in with her own cup of tea.

"Well," I began. "This adventure began many months ago. I received a letter from a legal firm in Ballina that my family has used for several generations. It seems that they had been trying to find my father for years and had just recently found out that he had died. Then they began looking for his next of kin."

"A lawyer, or I should say solicitor, by the name of Maureen called me. She was great to speak with. She told me that I had inherited my father's farm and that a neighbor had been using the farmland all of these years, and that he had petitioned for ownership. With the laws governing vacant land in Ireland, she was afraid that he would win the case and asked if it was possible for me to come over to Ireland and sort things out.

"That's true" Molly said, nodding her head. "Tis best if these things are handled in person."

"Unfortunately I had to laugh at her suggestion. There was no way I could afford a trip over. I explained that I was going on a long-awaited bus trip to Montana with a group, and couldn't back out at the last minute because it was paid for and I couldn't get a refund.

"I thought it over and decided that I couldn't afford to own land in Ireland. Heck, I couldn't even afford the airfare, never mind any back taxes, or things like that, so I asked her to try to find a relative who lived nearby who could use the land."

"And what did she think of that suggestion?" Molly asked.

"She sounded very doubtful but said that she would get on it right away and get back to me. I sent her a postcard from Montana and asked if she had had any luck finding anyone that I could turn the land over to, but I didn't get a response.

"Months later when I called her office, I was told that she was not available and that someone else was working my case. Well, I felt that something was wrong, but I didn't know what to do about it, and tried to forget about the land.

"Then Mary won the airline tickets in a contest and we began to make plans to come over, and hoped to speak with Maureen. We were both a little afraid to come to a foreign country. And there were many things to work out . . . like how on earth you get a passport so quick and everything. Then I remembered that in high school I had volunteered for a local senator, and people always asked him for help. The next thing I knew, we were on our way here." I stopped my long story and drank some more of my tea.

"So you won a 'contest'? Could you tell me a little about that?" Molly asked.

I told her all about it and she laughed and said something like "not in our time but his."

"Excuse me," I said, but Molly just smiled.

"Brilliant isn't it. I'm just marveling over the ways of the world. Tis a wonder, isn't it? Please, go on with your story. How did you find Mayo?"

"Well, we drove straight there from the airport, much to Mary's dismay."

In a very roundabout way, I told of the visit to the solicitor's office to meet the new lawyer who had been assigned my case. I told of the visit to the land and showed her what I found in the cottage. Then I spoke of our trip to the burial mound, and then I stopped, not sure of how to go on from there. I drank some more of my tea and waited for her to say something, but she didn't. *Okay*, I thought, *here goes.*

"Aunt Molly," I asked, "do you believe in faeries or leprechauns?"

She laid her head back against the couch and laughed out loud.

"Well, now, of course I do. What a thing to be asking an Irishwoman. It was not too long ago that I met a very handsome leprechaun and had a nice conversation with him, indeed I did."

"But how is that possible? How could they exist and no one knows anything about them?" I asked, and again got that beautiful laugh.

"Now, how can you say no one knows about them? Aren't they written about in every country in the world? Of course they are called by many names; Elves, Cluricauns, and Grogpch among others.

"Some of us are lucky to meet them, and others often hope

to. So tell me, why do you ask me such a question, my dear Bridget?"

I told her of my falling into the mound or someplace that was magical and speaking with a faerie and the head leprechaun. I also told her about the neighbor that wanted to take over my land, and the missing solicitor who was dead and who spoke with me. Well, sort of. I told of how the lawyer had been trying to help me find someone to take care of the land and keep it in the family. I ended my long story with the list of concerns I had, about how on earth I could be of help to find out who may have killed Maureen and keep my land in the family.

"Well it looks as if you have a lot on your plate right now. I think it would be wise to have a good night's sleep and we will sort it all out, in the morning."

"So you don't think that it's something I ate or inhaled that has caused all of these hallucinations?" I asked, still hopeful that none of this was real.

"No, Bridget, you have been given a great boon; you have been asked to help the wee people—and they very seldom ask us for anything these days. I think that they never would have asked, if they had not already believed you could accomplish this task. Now go on with you, and have your shower and a very good sleep. We will sort this all out in the morning," she said, as she rose to hug me good night as she had Mary earlier.

I made my way to the bedroom and picked up my shower bag from the pile of suitcases next to the bed. Mary was sound asleep with a travel guide open on her chest and her notebook and pen by her side.

She would never go anywhere without her notebook. Mary was a natural-born researcher. She was very curious about everything, and if she didn't know the answer, she would make a note of it and soon find it.

A shower seemed like a heavenly idea. I hoped I could relax enough to sleep. I climbed into the small shower stall and did some self-talk, a form of mediation that had worked in the past to help me relax, but for some reason it didn't work this time.

As I turned on the water, I did a mental cleansing, imagining the spray starting clean and beautiful at the top of my head, then turning gray, and finally black as it worked its way down my body taking away my tiredness, tension, fears, and apprehension. When I yawned, I realized that I was finally relaxed and ready for bed.

I quickly dried off, straightened up my mess, and walked into the hallway. I looked toward Aunt Molly's room, and saw that the lights were out. She was keeping Mick with her in her room, saying something about missing her little Ness, a West Highland Terrier she had had for many years. I could hear murmuring, and I smiled, happy that Mick could bring her some company. I yawned again and went to the comfortable bedroom where Mary was still asleep. I moved her guidebook and notebook to the end table and turned off her light.

I was able to see my way around the room with no problem, and I realized that there was a glow from the streetlight below. It was funny that I had forgotten we were in the city, maybe because I wasn't hearing noise and sirens blasting.

I smiled as I snuggled down under the covers and quickly thanked God for the day. I prayed that he would continue to watch over us. I fell sound asleep, and not even a dream disturbed me for the next few hours.

I woke to hear Aunt Molly talking. "Now, me boy, you remember what we talked about last night. You are going to stick with her day and night and don't give me any of your so-called shenanigans. Do you hear me? You owe her majesty a great deal and you have only to keep an eye out for now, just until she gets use to the idea of all of us. She may be a little too young and too independent for your liking, but she is family, and by God I will see you working in the coal pits if any bit of harm befalls her."

I wondered what had riled up Aunt Molly, and who she was talking with. Did she invite one of her sons over, and what the heck did she mean by 'too young'? I could no longer hear them talking, so I got up and dressed.

Mary must have woken early; she had made up her bed. It looked perfect, you could bounce a quarter on it, which was an old saying Sister Teresa would say as she taught us to make beds and clean up after ourselves. *Boy, I must have slept soundly, not to wake with Mary moving around the room.*

Interlude

 Molly looked over at her young guest. His English Irish heritage mixed with Roman blood showed in his looks and emphasized his very classical bone structure. Ah to be thirty years younger, she thought as she watched him pace across her bedroom floor. "Now there, My Lord, why are you in such a lather?

Mick answered through clenched teeth, "this was to be a simple task, they said, help her to uncover her own talents, help her be strong enough to solve a few simple challenges, they said. Are you aware of what they have in mind for Bridget?"

He gave no chance for Molly to answer. "How can a young girl from Brooklyn stop the Goddess of War? This is a task that is not possible for someone so young and inexperienced to accomplish. She is not strong, nor skilled enough. She will come to harm. I will not be a party to put a young lady in danger."

"You are forgetting who her ancestors are and mistaking personality for skill. Give her some time. Be with her and protect her. I don't believe she is ready to have you reveal your skills to her as yet My

Lord, but please don't let her out of your sight. No harm will come to her while you are with her."

"But will the strength of her ancestors be enough, I strongly doubt it. It is time I stand up to our queen. For starters I am going to ask around for another home for her to haunt."

"My Lord, I don't think that is very wise. Remember the task at hand. I think you have come to like my niece and want to sidetrack our queen, but you will not dissuade her."

*Chapter 8*

# Playing Tourist

As I entered the living room, I could hear Aunt Poly singing along with a song on the radio, but I couldn't find anyone else in the room. Maybe it was the radio I heard all along.

"Good morning, Aunt Molly. How are you this morning?" I asked.

She smiled. "I am fine, dear. Did you sleep well?" She asked as she hurried to the kitchen.

"I had a wonderful sleep, thank you. I don't usually sleep in. It must be the fresh air. What time is it anyway?"

"Well now," Aunt Molly said, as she checked the clock on the stove, "it is just past noon."

"Past *noon?*" I couldn't believe it; I had not slept that long in years. "I feel great. I thought I had had a good night's sleep; which is usually more like eight or nine hours, but holy cow! That means I slept fourteen hours. Good God, I never sleep that long."

"Now, dear, you needed the rest," she said, "with the flight and the driving and all."

*Yes,* I thought, *"and all."*

Looking around I asked, "Where is Mary? Has she started out to sightsee by herself?"

"Sure, now, that one was up with the birds. Not even a bite to eat and she was out the door. I gave her a map of the city and the bus schedule. She was planning a grand day for herself," Molly said, smiling.

"Wow, Mary didn't eat? That alone shows she was excited. I bet she fell asleep planning all the sights she would see today," I said, trying to sound good-natured, but I was feeling a little depressed. Heck, this was my first time in this city, and I didn't want to play detective. I wanted to sightsee also.

As if sensing my thoughts, Molly said, "Now come along and eat a bite of food, and afterward, we will also see the sights before we sort things out for the place in Mayo."

I perked up at the thought of putting off the problem in Mayo for another day, and soon we were heading out the door.

"Oh, no," I said. "I forgot, we can't take Mick on the bus. I will need to drive."

"And I would like to see someone stop a poor old blind lady and her seeing-eye dog," Molly said, while reaching for her sunglasses.

I had to laugh at the sight of my elderly little Aunt Molly being led around by a young pup in a too-big harness. But I have to admit he carried it off like a pro.

We had a wonderful time walking all around Dublin; I saw the beauty of the historical Trinity College, ogled the goods to be purchased on Grafton Street, and even took pictures of the Tart with the Cart, as the locals call the beautiful statue of Molly Malone wheeling her barrow.

We stopped for lunch at a large cafeteria on St. Andrew's

Street. Molly handed me the dark glasses and told me to watch Mick as she went to get our lunch.

Before I had a chance to argue, she was gone. I found a table in the corner, trying my best to be inconspicuous with Mick.

The restaurant was good sized, and the two-story tall window of glass gave the illusion of a much larger space. They must have space to seat a couple hundred people.

While I was worrying about some manager coming over and kicking us out, we were discovered by every child in the place. They came over to pet and play with Mick.

You could tell he loved the attention, and he loved kids. When he was tired of being petted, he did tricks for them. He stood on his hind legs, danced, rolled over, and even shook hands. He was amazing. I loved hearing the laughter and strong Irish accents of the children when they talked to Mick. I could tell that we both were enjoying their company.

Aunt Molly arrived with the food, and smiled at the children. "Be off with ye now," she told them. "Let the poor lady eat her meal in peace."

I looked down at my lunch and gasped. "There is no way in heaven I could eat all of this." The plate was piled high with roast beef, mashed potatoes, gravy, green beans, and a large pile of fresh baby potatoes, with their light golden skins still on. "I will gladly share half of this with Mick," I said, hopefully.

"Now, do you think I would be forgetting our Mick?" Aunt Molly asked as she placed a plate of food identical to my own on the floor under the table, and Mick began to devour it.

*Hate to question Irish customs but wouldn't dog food be better, they must feed the animals people food over here. Well he looks healthy.*

The roast beef could be cut with a fork, and the new potatoes were heavenly. The butter and cream in this country was better than I had ever tasted in my life, and now I added meat and potatoes to that list. No wonder they serve two kinds of potatoes, no one could pick just one.

I was merrily eating when I felt something hit on the side of my face lightly. *Hmm, that felt familiar.* Sure enough, when I looked down on the table, there was a wadded up piece of paper that looked suspiciously like the cover to a straw.

I looked around and spotted a red-headed little boy, about six, and his younger brother, giggling away. I gave them my best stern nun face and they stopped giggling and looked a little scared. Then I stuck out my tongue. They rolled off their chairs laughing. I had to laugh out loud at how angelic they looked. I knew the young mother trying to scold them sure had her hands full.

Through all of this, I felt as if I was being watched; I looked down to see Mick looking at me. *Doesn't he look funny; it's almost as if he was looking me over. Like the measuring look you'd get on a job interview.* My imagination is running wild. I scolded myself, and then I'm sure I heard someone say, *"Shows some promise,"* what's up with that?

I started to ask Molly if she heard anything but she was asking how I liked the food. I looked at my plate and was surprised to see that I'd eaten all that food.

"Molly, that was wonderful. Thank you very much."

"Sure, and you are very welcome," she said with a smile. "Now, what do you think of a walk in the park so that Mick here can have a little run?"

"That sounds great," I said. "I have not seen a park here yet. Is it very far?"

"No, just a few steps away. Ah, there is the bus now," Molly said, looking out the glass wall of the restaurant, and away she went.

I watched as she left the restaurant and crossed the street. I was in shock for a second, and then Mick bumped me with his head and we were running after her across two very wide lanes of traffic.

## Chapter 9
# Phoenix Park, Dublin

I quickly put on my glasses as I heard Molly say, for the benefit of the bus driver, and as a reminder to me: "There now, sweetie, just two steps up, ah, now, and there is a good girl. Ah, here is a kind young man sitting here that would be more than happy to give you his seat, now, wouldn't you?" Molly asked a guy with a sharp, purple and green Mohawk.

The guy looked at me and got up among the sound of chains rattling. I had to stare at the chains. They were wrapped around his neck, waist, and there was even a chain hanging from his nose draping over to his ear. *Yikes, that must hurt. I was going to get a nose ring but couldn't figure out how I would blow my nose?* His girlfriend, dressed identically, also got up and joined him near the back door.

As Molly sat next to me, she mumbled, "Now sure and keep ya yap shut. You don't want them to know you are a bloody foreigner."

I had to smile at that. Molly wasn't as nonchalant as she first appeared. It must have been hard for her to ask the tough-looking teens to move. So, with the warning to keep quiet and the help of the dark sunglasses, I spent the time looking at the people in the bus.

I felt as if I was on a bus in the States. There were a variety of people, blue-collar folks coming or going to work, and a few strangely dressed teens searching for their personal identity. Also a group of young girls from a Catholic school all dressed in the same uniforms. That was a sight you don't see very often. *Hmm,* I thought, *they look better in their uniforms than I did in my white blouse and plaid skirt.*

I felt so comfortable. I heard a low murmur and realized that I had been stroking Mick for the last ten minutes. His eyes were closed, and he almost sounded like he was purring. No, that couldn't be. *Cats* purr.

Well, he sounded content, and I think that small sound and act of stroking him added to my sense of peace. Now I knew why so many people had pets. Just touching them puts you in a relaxed state of mind.

We got off the bus in the middle of a very large park. Now, I have been to Central Park in New York, but I would say that at a glance Phoenix Park in the middle of Dublin looked much larger.

We walked for a while, each lost in our own thoughts. We fed the pigeons with a bag of bread that Molly pulled from her large carry-all. We sat on a brightly painted bench and just enjoyed the sun shining on our faces; it was a perfect day.

Quietly, Molly reached over and took both my hands in hers.

"What are you feeling about all that has occurred since you stepped foot in Ireland?"

"What am I feeling?" I asked. "I really wish I could just say that I'm happy to be here, but to tell you the truth, I'm on over-load. I'm feeling happy at being here and meeting my family, sad that I had not met you all much sooner, and a little angry that I didn't have you all as a part of my life before.

"Of course, I'm very sad that I can't just be a tourist and enjoy the sights. I'm scared that I have been asked to be Nancy Drew and solve a mystery.

"Why me? Why does all of the responsibility always fall to me? I really don't understand why I need to solve a murder and why it's so important to save my land?"

"Well now Bridget, it is not for the likes of me to know the thinking of the Fae folk but what I am thinking is that this is a test. You see you are of their blood and being so you must have some gifts that you have not used yet. Perhaps when you use some of those talents to solve the murder and save your family land then you will become closer to your Fae heritage," Molly suggested.

"But I'm so *tired* of being the strong one, why *me?*" I asked with a great deal of self-pity. "Aunt Molly, I'm so sorry, I don't know what came over me. I don't usually blurt out my feelings. I've never done that before; there must be something in the air over here. I usually am much more in control."

"Now, there," she said, reaching for an old-fashioned hanky. "You have been introduced to many new things all at once. And didn't I ask you how you were feeling, and didn't you just answer me honestly?" She leaned over and wiped my tears. The gentle-ness and kind tone of her voice made me want to cry more.

"Thank you, Aunt Molly. You're wonderful."

"Hush now," she said, handing me the beautiful lace-edged

hanky that was embroidered with what looked like a Celtic circle symbol.

"You keep that with you, and remember now that you have family fighting alongside you. You do know that we are never really alone, don't you?" she asked.

I nodded but wondered at her words.

"I believe that you have been given a miraculous gift," Molly said, with a bit of wonder in her voice.

I looked at my aunt, and saw her eyes shining with unshed tears.

"Do you realize how very few people are open enough to receive the gift of knowing that the faerie folk are with us . . . let alone meet them? You not only know that they really exist—you have met with the head of the leprechauns and the great Queen Geraldine, the leader of the entire faerie world. To let that happen, they must really believe in you."

"Believe in me," I repeated. "Believe in me to do what?"

"Sure, now," she said, ignoring my question. "They only pick humans that have not closed their mind to the unseen. Humans, who have within them the desire to do great things, I would say that you can meet this challenge. You can overcome your fears and doubts, and become the strong, self-confident Irishwoman we all know that you are.

"Now you do have a choice, you know. You can always choose not to help the people of Erie. You could choose to be a tourist, return home, and leave your family land and a murderer to their own fate."

After a few seconds of silence, she fired the full arsenal of guilt. "You have the choice to turn your back on those who care for you and have chosen you, among millions, to aid them in their time of need." With that said, Aunt Molly gathered her carry-all and stood up.

I started to follow, but she gestured for me to stay sitting. "Just sit awhile, and when you make your decision, walk over that way for a bit, and you will find my place," she said, pointing north along the path. She reached down to hug me good-bye and was off. Gone was the leisurely stroll we've enjoyed earlier. Aunt Molly was back to her city stride, and I wondered if she ever really slowed down for very long.

I continued to watch her and marveled at her long, powerful walk, and the way she held her head up. She always walked with purpose, her blond hair shinning in the sun, and her small petite muscled body denying her age. I hope someday I will have that much energy and enthusiasm for life.

What was that she said? *"You can always choose not to help the people of Erie; you can choose to be a tourist, return home, and leave your family land and a murderer to their own fate?"* Hah, some folks think the Jewish mothers know how to use guilt. Well, they have never met an Irishwoman. How do I walk away now? Not only would I be letting down my family, but all of Ireland . . . *good grief!*

Well, now what? It seems Molly thinks I was picked to handle this problem. Someone thinks I can do it, so I guess I'd better just do it. Great, now I sound like a Nike commercial. Just do it. Hah! Do what? I don't even know where to start.

Mick jumped up on the seat vacated by Molly and snuggled into my side. I put my arm around him and snuggled into him, wanting that sense of peace I felt on the bus. Yes, I know, I will do whatever I can do to find the murderer and save my land. But right now, I will just relax, enjoy the sun, the sound of children playing in the background, and enjoy holding Mick.

I have missed so much by not owning a dog. Mick feels so good with his head on my chest and his hard little body pressed tight against me. Mick let out a deep sigh. *I think he enjoys snuggling as much as I do, I smiled.*

## Chapter 10
# Bridget hears from Mick

I felt so good that I must have dozed off for a few minutes. I woke up when I felt Mick jump up. "Hey, Mick, what is the problem?" Then I noticed a gang of punks headed our way and prepared to make a run for it.

*What on earth was I thinking? This is a city, and it's getting dark. The children have left, and here I'm alone on a bench, with just a puppy. In Brooklyn, that's like wearing a sign, dummy here, mug me,* I stood and began to pull on Mick's lease as he growled at the gang of boys. I could've sworn I heard him say to the ringleader, "Leave this park. This is not a night to be out. Treat the other kids to a show and a burger."

What was that? *Animals can't speak,* I thought. I looked at the boys in astonishment. The kid with long spiked white-blonde hair, who looked to be the leader of the pack, put his hand up, and signaled them to stop.

"Hey guys," Blondie said to the others. "Let's cut out of here and take in a show. That dog looks mean." He laughed and turned around. When he began to walk in the opposite direction, his buddies looked puzzled but quickly followed.

"Talk, oh, my Gawd, Mick, did you just talk?" I yelled. But I did hear him in my head *"Now please calm down Bridget, this is not the way I was going to introduce myself, but action was needed. And how on earth are you hearing me?"*

I sat back down with a bang. "That was you. I heard you! Did you speak or what? It can't be you, but I heard a voice, or thought I heard it."

*"Bridget, animals are intelligent, feeling beings. They communicate by exchanging thoughts, using body language, vocalizations, marking, and so on. Because animals cannot speak in words, most humans believe that they cannot think."*

"But you're *a dog!*" I argued. "You don't speak. How can you think or reason?"

*"Most animals might argue that because humans speak, they have lost the ability to think!"*

"But you're a dog," I repeated stubbornly.

*"Yeah,"* he agreed wryly. *"I've noticed. So maybe we could get past that."*

"Who or what are you?" I asked but didn't wait for a reply. "I thought you might have been a gift to bring me comfort, but your here to protect me, aren't you? You're like a Lassie that can talk."

*"Well now . . ."* Mick began.

"Don't you 'well now' me!" I shouted. "Why didn't you tell me that you could talk? Well, not that you're really talking, I'm talking and you're answering in my head . . . what is that? No, don't answer. I have so many questions to ask you, and I don't know where to begin."

*"Happily, Bridget, there is another, more sophisticated, in-depth option*

*available to us instead of shouting. It is telepathic communication. Telepathy is defined, in the dictionary, as communication of facts, feelings, and impressions, between mind and mind at a distance,"* Mick said, in a snooty voice.

"Whatareyoutalkingabout? I don't understand!" I shouted again.

*"If you would please just be quiet for a minute, then I could explain myself, and please, stop your shouting. You will have the Garda here in no time. All you have to do is to think what you want to say, and I will hear you,"* Mick said in my head. *"Besides, you have the loudest, most scattered thoughts that I have ever come across. There is no way I could not hear you.*

*"In answer to your question, I'm a gift from Graa . . . Geraldine and Padraig. I have been asked to teach you a few things,"* he began.

"Yeah, right," I said. "I heard Molly this morning, and by the way she sounded, you must owe a big debt to Padraig, and he is making you help me."

*"Do you want to hear what I have to say, or do you just want to hear your own thoughts on the matter? It is up to you,"* he said.

*He sounds rather uppity*, I thought. *He can sure get on his high horse, even though he is a wee little dog.* I laughed.

*"That does it,"* Mick said, and he stormed off, at least for a couple of feet, until he came to the end of the leash. That made him even madder, so he sat down.

"Good grief, it looks like you're pouting. How can a puppy pout?" I asked between laughs. "Now, Mick, be honest—how can I *not* laugh? Don't you see the humor in this? You know, like Lois Lane had Superman, and Batman had Robin, I have a puppy. Or is it Super Puppy?"

"Okay, okay, come on" I said, as I watched him hang his head. "I didn't mean it. Go ahead and tell me the whole story." I waited, but heard nothing. "Mickey, my little cutie pie, please now, don't be as stubborn as a mule." I laughed. "Sorry, I can't seem to stop the animal jokes. But, if I needed a helper, then why not a leprechaun or a faerie? At least *they* could fight someone for me. Are you really a leprechaun or faerie?"

"*No,*" he answered, still hanging his head.

"Now don't get me wrong. Your mind-control act is really neat, and it's nice to be able to talk with someone all the time . . . but if I get in trouble, what on earth could you do to help me out?"

Mick let go a deep, angry growl, and started to pull at the leash.

"Okay, I get it. Just like a guy. I hurt your feelings and now I get the silent treatment." *Good grief, I'm talking to a dog and upset that I'm not getting an answer. Okay, am I really losing it, or is it because I have met the Queen of the Faeries and the Head of the Leprechauns, that a talking dog seems normal?*

I laughed as I got up from the park bench to start the walk back to Aunt Molly's place. "Maybe Molly will have some answers for me." I hoped.

As was my way, I started to ramble. "Okay, Mick my boy, how do you get your thoughts across to someone without words? Still no answer, huh?

"Now that I think about it, most folks can get their thoughts across without words. When Mary gives you one of her looks, you sure know that it's best to just leave her alone or suffer the consequences."

We passed a couple of teens dressed all in black. I looked at them and got back a look that was definitely a "get lost" look. "You know, Mick, I think we teens have that 'communication with just a look' down pat, don't you?" I asked, but still no response.

"Your a dog! Well, a gifted, talking dog, but how can you get a message across with just a look? I heard you growl and saw your mean look but . . . Okay, I give up," I said, when he let go with another low, menacing growl. I was quiet for the next mile or so, but I couldn't stop thinking about this talking dog.

I stopped walking, and looked down at him.

"Okay, Mick, I admit humans can send messages to others with a look. But you can do it by sending your thoughts. But it wasn't only your thoughts, was it? You hypnotized that boy to leave us alone, didn't you? That's it, isn't it? You can control minds! How freaky is that? Is that how you got someone to put you in the back of my car? But wait. My car was locked. How . . ."

*"Don't you think that we had better get moving? It is getting dark, and you don't know your way around yet."*

"Well, Mick, I will take that as an 'I'm not going to answer you, so stop asking questions,' interruption. But you're right. We had better get going."

We started walking in the direction I had thought Molly had indicated, and I kept up my one-sided conversation. "Hey, did you see the size of that guy? I don't think he was scared of you. Well, what would you do—bite his ankle?" I said, and laughed so hard the tears started to come. It didn't help when I heard Mick growl again.

Okay, I knew that I wasn't being very nice with my animal jokes, but I guess the stress of the last few days had gotten to me. I either cry or laugh when stressed out, and I really prefer to laugh. Right now, I had the picture in my head of my fifteen-pound red and white spaniel companion biting the ankle of the six-foot four-inch, two hundred pound bully.

The more I thought about it, the harder I laughed, and the harder I laughed, the more indignant Mick became. His long, floppy, rust-colored ears were back from his face as far as they could be; he was walking so stiffly he looked like pictures I had seen of a Pointer. That image started me smiling again, until I saw the look in those beautiful amber eyes; heck, how could amber look so cold? There was so much cold in that look it could freeze a volcano. *Hmm, Mick has no sense of humor.*

After ten blocks of the silent treatment, I stopped and looked around. We were getting into a commercial area, and I realized that I was lost. I looked at Mick, and I swear that dog was grinning.

*Okay, so Mr. Fluffball got even. He led me ten blocks in the wrong direction; I will just turn around and not give him the satisfaction of saying anything,* I thought.

"Fluffball?" he shouted in my head. *"Who is the one with the leash leading the poor little doggie around?"*

Well, I wasn't going to give the hound the glory of leading me home. I spotted a lady and stopped her to ask directions. She was taller than I and had beautiful, natural blond hair and cornflower-blue eyes that matched the look of the two twin boys she had in tow.

I asked her how I would find the Guinness brewery, and she very pleasantly said that she was walking that way herself and would I like her to walk with me?

I could feel Mick pull against the leash, and I knew he wanted me to move, but why? It couldn't be the lady. She was really sweet and had a wonderful smile. Then I looked at the two boys, around age six, each with the largest, stickiest lollipop that I had ever seen. They politely asked their mother if they could pet the puppy.

*Ah, revenge is really sweet,* I thought as I laughed to myself.

"Boys, my dog's name is Mick and he just loves to be petted," I said, and they did.

Soon Mick was licking his coat, and I was laughing again, as his hair stood up in clumps from the sugar sticky sweetness of the lollipops.

Ah, if looks could kill, the look I was getting from Mick was priceless. I laughed again. I don't think that I had laughed so hard in a long time. Mick was fun to be around. He may just be a dog, but he was great company.

*Chapter 11*

# More Family

Soon we were back at the entrance to Phoenix Park, and I found out along the way that Evelyn was very friendly. We spoke as if we've known each other all our lives. She asked if I was going to Guinness' to take the tour. I said no, I'm visiting an aunt who lived near there at St. James Flats.

"By any chance would her name be Molly?" She laughed.

I stopped walking and just stared at her.

"Yes," I said, and she laughed some more.

"That is brilliant. Me mam is always going on about the fact that there are no coincidences, and after all these years, she may be right. I am your cousin, and Molly is my mother. The boys and I were on the way over to meet you."

I looked down at Mick, but he wouldn't look at me at all. *I wonder if he walked this way on purpose. Nah, he couldn't have known, could he?*

We arrived back at the apartment to find both Aunt Molly and Mary going over a copy of the *Irish Times*. After introductions and my telling of our miraculous meeting, Mary told us what they had been discussing: the newspaper was reporting a bombing at London's Heathrow Airport and blaming it on the Irish Republic Army, but the leaders of the IRA were denying the connection.

"That reporter is not aware of the truth." Molly said. "There was always a radical group calling themselves the IRA, which is not the true members. In years past, when the real IRA was responsible, they were the first to admit it."

I had read that for the past twenty years the IRA had been working to build up the economy in Ireland and keep the peace, so much so, that now Ireland was called the "Celtic Tiger." I also didn't believe that they would be retaliating for past grievances and thought she may be right. But then why would the paper want to blame the Irish people?

Mary continued reading the article to us. The reporter went on to say that terrorist activity had been increasing over the past ten years, but yesterday's bombing was the worst he had ever seen.

"But that conflicts with what I have been reading. It doesn't make sense," I said.

I could tell that Aunt Molly was very upset, so I decided to change the subject. I mentioned that I was starving after such a long walk. My comment had the desired effect. Both Molly and Evelyn jumped up. Molly went to the kitchen, and Evelyn turned and said, "Boys wash up before your tea and leave off tormenting that poor dog." then she followed Molly to the kitchen.

Of course Mary and I offered to help out with the preparations, but we were told to put our feet up and take a rest. They would call us when dinner was ready.

I asked Mary what she had done with herself that day. She became very excited, and told me of seeing Trinity College and the *Book of Kells*. She said that she had had no problem getting around and that she had met some great people.

I asked Mary why she thought Aunt Molly was so upset about the article in the paper.

"I don't know . . . maybe she thinks that too many people will believe what they read. The English and Irish are getting along great now after so many years of conflict."

"I have been thinking about that. What if the papers are wrong in what they are reporting? I wonder who wants the wrong news to get out," I said.

Mary looked at me as if I had grown horns.

"What?" I asked.

"You're interested in world news all of a sudden?"

"Well, it's not just 'world news' anymore. This is my family that might get hurt. Molly is so great; I don't like to see her worried. She does look worried, doesn't she?" I said. I felt that Molly hated all forms of violence. I believed that she had seen way too much of it in her lifetime. I also had a strong feeling that she may have had many friends in the IRA. It will take awhile to explain all of these strong feelings to Mary; I had better wait until we were alone.

I didn't get time to think about it for long; the boys were asking us questions about America and wanted to know if we've ever been to a McDonald's. There was a new McDonald's restaurant in Dublin, and they said they would use their money to take us there.

"'Tis a grand place Aunt Bridget, me brother and I will be happy to take you both there," said Kirin. I think it was Kirin but it might have been Darrin, it was difficult to tell them apart.

They were so excited; they were a joy to watch. I wondered

if Mickey Dee's had the same effect all over the world when it opened a new store.

Molly and Evelyn loaded the kitchen counter buffet style.

"It is ready now, come help yourselves," announced Molly.

We dished up some excellent chicken, potatoes, and fresh carrots.

"Molly, thank you so much, this is the best chicken I have ever tasted." I said.

Mary agreed, "This is wonderful, thank you both."

Our comments were greeted with dead silence.

"Molly had purchased turkey for you both because we were told that all Americans loved turkey." Evelyn explained.

Mary and I looked again at the size of the bird, and we were in shock.

"No wonder it tastes so great— being the size of one of our chickens, it probably had no growth hormones." Mary said.

We laughed and explained our mistake. We all had a great time, talking about family and our trip. I could tell they were interested in all things American. We talked for several hours on fun subjects like shopping, food, movies, and all things not stressful. When it was time to leave, Molly called a taxi for Evelyn and the boys.

It was only a little past nine, and I was yawning.

"Why don't we all make an early night of it." Molly suggested and I didn't argue.

"I can't believe how tired I am," I said, attempting to stifle a yawn. "I think I will go to bed early. It must be all of the walking we did today."

"Good night, Aunt Molly," I said, as I leaned over to kiss her good night. I patted Mick on the head and told him good night.

Mary did the same and went to the bedroom to schedule tomorrows sight-seeing.

It didn't take long to shower and get ready for bed. For some strange reason, I was more relaxed that night than I had been the previous night. I didn't even try to analyze why. As soon as my head hit the pillow I was sound asleep.

*Chapter 12*

# Gifts

Mary had once again left the apartment before I opened my eyes. She must be really enjoying herself, I thought. Usually I wake up to her banging doors and grumbling until she had her morning caffeine. Waking up to peace and quiet is a joy.

Aunt Molly was sitting with Mick when I came into the living room. Molly looked at me and smiled. "Ah, now, the dead arose and appeared to many."

I smiled and was able to say good morning, although I felt as if I had been hit in the chest. It had been a long time since I heard Grandma Prendergast greet her children that way, after they had stayed in bed too long. It was always said with love and humor. Right here, right now, it felt just right.

"There now, have a seat. Breakfast is all ready."

"Thank you, Aunt Molly, breakfast sounds great. I'm starving." I turned to Mick. "And a top of the morning to you, Mick my boy, have you been talking to Aunt Molly?"

"Ah, is that the way it is then. You have officially been introduced to our Mick, is it?" Molly asked me with her hands on her hips. She was no longer smiling.

I heard Mick make a noise. I ignored him and told Molly about the guys in the park yesterday and how Mick had saved the day.

She nodded again without smiling. "Well, I guess you had better eat. You have a busy day ahead of you." She turned and walked into the kitchen.

I looked over at Mick and whispered, "Did I do anything wrong?"

*"No, Bridget, it isn't you who is troubling Molly. I am the one you could say is in the doghouse."*

I laughed at Mick's comment. I don't know how, with all of this paranormal stuff going on, but I felt happier than I had been for a very long time.

"Why? What did you do wrong?" I asked Mick.

*"Well, you could say that I was just an eejit. I had forgotten who your parents were. I should have realized that you would be able to hear the thoughts I broadcasted to the boys. My task was to watch out for you, but not to—how do you Yanks say it?--blow my cover just yet."*

"So I gather that eejit is Irish for idiot." I laughed. "And why would it hurt for me to know that a talking dog was watching out for me?" I asked. "I sort of like it, you know. Especially now, that I have gotten over the shock. It's nice to talk over all of the things running around in my head. Especially since I'm still not sure if I'm crazy or not."

Any answer that he might have given me was postponed, for at that moment, Molly came back into the room with a huge tray of food.

"Aunt Molly, have you ever met Grace?"

"Many years ago, when I was much younger than you are now. I was lost and since I always loved the story of Grace, I called out to her for help. She appeared and asked me to vow not to reveal her presence, for only a few are really blessed to know the faeire world. I have always felt that I was a friend and would be called upon if needed. Now, enough with that, your breakfast will be getting cold."

We had a great meal including fresh ham, eggs, biscuits, fried potatoes, and of course, tea. *I could really love living here*, I thought. *It's okay to eat like this when you walk all over town and not sit at a desk all day.*

After breakfast I helped Molly with the dishes and cleaning the kitchen. Feeling that Mick and I could both use a long walk after that great breakfast, I attached his leash for appearance's sake, and headed toward Stephens Square.

"Will you be okay on your own this morning Bridget?" Aunt Molly asked. I am off to visit some folks about that article in the paper yesterday.

"No problem, I really need to come up with a plan or two. I will take Mick for a long walk."

━━━━◦《◉》◦━━━━

"I have to admit that there is a great advantage to being able to talk with just our thoughts. This way, no one can hear me speaking to a dog," I said, trying to get Mick to talk to me. After breakfast, he again had started giving me the silent treatment, and I really didn't like it.

"Bridget, I am not 'giving you the silent treatment' this morning. I am trying to put the right words together to get you to realize the gifts you have been given but have very seldom used."

"Now, you're a good one to talk, Mick. I know that you have

the gift of mind control, and yet you have not brought Maureen's murderer to justice. Why is that? I just don't understand. Why don't you and Padraig just, you know, just mind control people to do what you want them to do—like turn themselves in to the police?" I asked.

"First of all, Bridget, our police are called the Garda over here, and you cannot get people to do what you wish them to do. We must never apply our will to anyone. For you know that to coerce others by physical means is slavery. To coerce them by mental means is also slavery; the only difference is the method. To get others to do what you want is not right."

"But what if you know it's for their good? Then can you use mind control?" I asked.

"No, not even if you think it is for their own good, because how do you know what is for a person's own good?"

"I will give you that point. I don't know if it's for their good. But what about keeping them and others from getting hurt?"

"Aye, we can do that, and as you saw in the park, I was able to talk those lads into a better course of action. But even that type of thing we try to stay away from, for we do not really know what is meant to happen. What if it will turn out good for someone in the long run?" he said.

*Hah. I can't see how getting mugged would help anyone.* "Okay, Mick, I have another question. If I have the ability to use this mind control you speak of but I can't use it to coerce others to do my will, what good is it? I mean, how on earth am I to get the resources I need to be of any help in finding Maureen's murderer?"

"Now, there is one of two things that you need to learn. I would say that you are bright lass, and learn quickly. Why not try a little experiment? I would like you to learn to quiet your thoughts for as long as you can," Mick requested.

"What do you mean quiet? There are many times that I don't say anything for a long time," I said, sounding pouty even to my own ears.

"Bridget, please let me re-word that request. Try being quiet, I mean, not only in your speech but also in your thoughts. That is a little more difficult to do. You yourself must admit that there is many a time that your thoughts are running around in your head a hundred miles a minute." He paused as if to give me time to think that over.

"I would like you to try to be still. Look at a flower, and just be with the flower, or tree, or bird. Pick anything that you are drawn to. Just be with it, and do not try to think about its name, how it looks, or how it feels. Just be still. Do you think you could do that?"

"Of course, anyone can do that. It sounds silly, but I will try." I looked around, but with the noise of the traffic and people walking around us, I couldn't seem to concentrate on any one thing.

"Let's walk to that little park over there and have a seat on the bench for a minute," I said. We crossed St. Stephens Street and sat on a wooden bench that had been placed under an ancient tree. Mick jumped up alongside me and just looked at me as he waited for me to digest all that he had been telling me.

"Okay, I will show you that I can be still," I said, sounding much braver than I felt. I looked up through the tree branches and decided to concentrate on the sun. It was shinning bright and felt so good. I hadn't noticed how good it felt. Maybe Mick was right, maybe I needed to notice the things around me more. Maybe I had been doing everything wrong all of my life. I should not worry about everything. I should pay more attention to things around me.

"Bridget, stop right now!" Mick shouted in my head. "Do you realize what you are doing? You have not stopped your thoughts. Worse yet, you are belittling yourself for something that you have done in the past. That sounds like it is a very familiar pattern with you. Now, try it again. This time, please, try not to think about anything. I know that it is hard at first, but you will come to feel that you have rested for hours with only a few minutes of stillness."

I began to feel bad about doing it wrong, but I caught myself and looked again at the sun. This time, I was able to still my thoughts for at least a couple of seconds. As soon as I started thinking again, I smiled. "This is really hard. Do people actually do this, or is it only wee folk and talking dogs that can be still?"

Mick made a noise that sounded something like a laugh, but closer to an old creaky door that had not been opened very often. "Now, Bridget, I know that you work hard to be positive in your communications with other folks. All I am asking for you to do for now, other than learn to be still, is to go easy on yourself. Give yourself some positive talk. I think you did very well with your first lesson on being still. You would be wise to begin to watch the words that you speak, not only to yourself, but to others. Words have special power. You speak to me of 'mind control.' Now that has a negative tone. We use the term 'willpower.'

"We all have the power to control our own will. To many people, the term mind control sounds as if others have the power to control us. The truth is, if our minds were our own, then no one could control us."

"I will try, but it will take some doing; my mind is always

racing a hundred miles an hour."

"I know," he said, with a warm smile in his voice.

We got up from the bench and walked the path alongside the River Liffey. Mick was quiet, but of course my mind was racing again with thoughts of how on earth I would save my land and help find Maureen's murderer. I am not Kinsey Millhouse, or even Nancy Drew.

My negative thoughts were interrupted again by Mick.

"Bridget, you cannot apply your will to others, but you must begin to believe that all that you need will be provided. You only need to be grateful for what you already have."

"Oh, do you mean just use a positive mental attitude?"

"That is a part of using the gift, but think of it this way: being positive or grateful for all that you have, is not something that you will do once a month, or Heaven forbid, only on your Thanksgiving holiday. Let me try explaining it this way: Einstein proved that everything in the universe is energy. Your thoughts, feelings, and beliefs determine the vibration and frequency of your energy.

"As you focus on the positive aspects of life, and think, speak, and feel positively, you are transforming your energy frequency to one of the most powerful and highest frequencies of all. In other words, you will magnetize to you the energy of people, circumstances, and events that will bring good into your life."

"So by saying that all good will come to me, you mean that the money I need to support Mary and me while we're in Ireland, will just come to me?"

"If money is what you need. Now it may not be. I have heard you mention money a great deal. Poverty is foremost in your mind. Poverty is what you direct all of your energy toward.

Therefore, poverty is what you bring into your life; it will be what you manifest. Bridget, you may not realize it, but you speak of being without funds, in one way or another, a dozen times a day. You speak of being poor in the past, you worry about being poor in the future, and you worry about needing money today. Your life is filled with negative thinking. The negative things we experience in life are often caused by turning away from all the good that there is.

"How can I say this so you will understand? I know that it is not easy to change a lifelong habit. Imagine that the sun is sending out positive energy to us. You experience the full effect of the sun when you are facing it, but if you turn away, you will no longer receive its effects. Positive energy operates identically to the sun. It is always there and always available, sending out good things to you. But when you worry, as you do, or even complain, blame, criticize, or have any negative emotion, you turn away from all that is good. The more you give power to the thoughts of poverty, the more you lose the energy."

"Hey, whadayamean? I'm positive," I said out loud, and startled a few passersby. I smiled at them and walked a little faster.

"Yes you are, but you need to have it fill your life. For example, even now, while I am speaking with you, you are worrying about paying to change the date on your return airline tickets," Mick said, sounding frustrated.

Well, he did lose me a little as he went on and on. "How do I force myself to think only positive thoughts?" I asked, still not believing this crazy dog.

"'Force' is a negative term. Think of all that I have said and we will make it our daily routine to take a walk together and discuss various issues that may interest you."

— 119 —

I could just see myself trying to explain any of this to Mary.

"Okay," I said. "Let's head back to Aunt Molly's. Mary may be home, and I think it's time I tell her what is going on. You're right, I do tend to remember her grumpy times, and instead of sharing my fears with her because I don't want to be told I'm being silly, or, worse, shouted at, I tend to try to take on everything myself. I really am grateful for Mary's friendship over the years. I did open up to her about my nightmares, and she listened. Maybe I can talk to her about leprechauns. I hope so. Hey, without her, I never would've gotten to Ireland to find that I can communicate with a hairy dog," I laughed.

The corner of Mick's mouth twitched, but the movement was so brief I couldn't tell whether he had smiled or sneered.

## Interlude

"Padraig, I am staying close to Bridget as you both ordered...... ah, suggested. But I cannot help but be concerned for her friend, Mary. She is very inquisitive and I believe that she may be getting involved in areas that do not concern her."

"You are correct My Lord. We have been keeping a watch on her and she is about to deliver a new test for our Bridget that we did not foresee. Tis no matter for we are certain that our girl will be able to take care of anything that comes her way."

"Please don't say it is another task." Mick groaned.

"The more a brain is used for good, the healthier it is. We both know that. Way too much time is used, dwelling on things that have an adverse affect on the body. Helping others, especially trying to solve a problem, keeps the mind off of self and any possible negativity."

"Will she be in danger?"

"Not that we can foresee, although you know our gifts are limited. Sit and we will tell you what we can see in store for Mary and our Bridget."

*Chapter 13*

# Compare Notes

Both Mary and I were quiet that night as we had dinner with Molly. We listened to Molly tell us about Dublin, about the growth and challenges they have had since joining the European Union. Soon Molly also was quiet.

After dinner she announced, "I will take care of the washing up. Now, why don't you both take Mickey for a walk in the park?"

We agreed and soon found ourselves on a park bench.

"Bridget," said Mary, "I have to tell you what I found out today."

Thinking that Mary was just going to tell me more Irish history, I cut in. "I have got to get this over with, I know that you will not believe anything that I'm going to tell you, but I will say it anyway. If you decide to lock me up, go ahead and I won't blame you."

"Bridget I know that there is something that you're not telling me. Ever since seeing your father's house you have been acting weird. The only reason I can think of to keep anything from me would be to protect me from something, but I can't figure out what that could be. To start with I know that you weren't lying in the rain next to the mound for too long, your clothes were not that wet. Why did you make up a story? Where were you? The only thing I could come up with was that you were taken by aliens."

I laughed at my friend who was writing a Sci-Fi novel and said, "Aliens, you mean little green men? Well you're almost right."

She didn't even smile so I could tell she had much more that she wanted to say and wouldn't be interrupted.

"I'm your friend and I'm here to help you though all of this, but how am I supposed to do that if you're keeping secrets from me? This whole trip is bringing your father back into your life big time. Hey, your dad alienated everyone around him with his drinking, including me. When Mom took you in twelve years ago after he died, you were a basket case. But even though you're only a few months older than me, you have always acted as if you were responsible for me. Well, I'm not that little girl anymore; I don't need you to protect me from this, whatever it is."

"I'm sorry, you're right." I looked over at a now puzzled Mary and began my story from our first day in Mayo. I told her everything: of the faerie mound on the land, up to finding out that Mick was a special dog sent by the faerie to help me solve the murder and keep the land.

Mary looked at me and just kept shaking her head. "Do you hear what you're saying, Bridget? You know that this is just not possible. There is no such thing as a talking dog!" she shouted.

I had to laugh. "Well, that's a mild response from you. I tell you all of that, about murder, leprechauns, and faeries. I expected you to be screaming at me by now, but all you respond to is a talking dog."

"Okay, Mick, speak to Mary!" I ordered but got no response. "Mick, go ahead and talk to Mary," I repeated. There was still no response from Mary, so I knew he wasn't cooperating. "What the heck kind of game are you playing, Mick? Talk to her now."

"*All in good time, Bridget, let Mary settle into the idea a little bit first, and when she is ready and needs to hear, then she will,*" Mick said in my head.

I looked over at Mary, and she was staring at Mick now, shaking her head. "I don't hear anything, Bridge. Heck, he isn't even moving his mouth."

"He doesn't move his mouth, he just sort of talks to your head. You hear him like you do your own thoughts. Okay, don't look at me like that, I mean it. Geraldine and Padraig both have the same gift," I explained.

"*Gift*, I think you've had too much bloody Irish tea! Really Bridge faeries and leprechauns? What next, the Loch Ness Monster? You have lost it big time, girlfriend."

*Well, I guess Mick is right. Mary is not ready.* I sighed to myself.

"Okay, I will let it pass for now. Oh, and *Miss Smarty Pants*, Nessie is Scottish. Tell me what your news is, and I will try to get Mick to talk to you. Heck, I've even heard him talk to Molly."

I caught the amazed look on Mary's face. "Well, to be honest, I heard Molly talk, and I didn't really hear Mick say anything at that time, but I think she was talking with him."

"Yea, I get it, the head talk stuff like you said. Bridget, everyone talks to dogs, but dogs don't talk back. Get it?" Mary said, looking sad as if she had lost her best friend to the halls of insanity. "And here I thought that *I* was the science fiction writer."

"Okay, okay, what's your news?" I said to change the subject.

"Well, today I met . . ." Mary began then stood up to pace in front of the bench and began fidgeting with her ponytail. I just waited. From years of knowing Mary, I could tell that she was thinking over what she was about to say, and all that I said.

She was frowning about something; I wondered what had happened to her. "Out with it, Mary, what are you so worried about telling me? Did you spend all of your money?"

"No, it's nothing like that. It's that I just realized my story may sound a bit fanciful also. And that maybe this is the land of interesting experiences. Who knows what's real, and what isn't. The myths and legends that are written in so many countries may have been based on some truth, and maybe it's possible. But, Bridget, really? A talking dog?"

"So are you telling me, girlfriend," I said, "that you may give me my leprechaun and queen of the faeries, but you will not give me a *male* dog with communication skills?" I looked at her and we both burst out laughing.

"Well, you have to admit, Bridge, *male* and *communication skill* is an oxymoron," Mary said, and we laughed some more.

I could hear Mick groan at our girlish humor and laughed harder.

"Okay, this is *crazy*. I will try to have an open mind, but it might take me a bit. Things have been very interesting since coming to Ireland." She got that far away look and became quiet again.

"Okay Mary, if you don't stop thinking so hard you will get frown lines. So enough hard thinking time and tell me already. What happened to you today?"

"Okay, here goes," Mary started. "Do you remember how upset Molly was over the report of the IRA bombing in the newspaper?

"Knowing you, I figured you would look into it. I keep telling you that you should be an investigative reporter, you missed your calling."

"You also warn me of what dangers my nosiness leads to. This time you may be right."

"Okay already, out with it, I'm dying here."

"Well this morning I waited for the bus and looked around at the people standing around. Whenever they caught me looking at them they would smile and say good morning. These people are friendly. There is something about Ireland that makes me feel safe. I wonder what it is. What's different here?"

When Mary got no response to her stalling tactics, she continued.

"Bus Eireann arrived. I sat down, took out my notebook to write down my thoughts." Mary reached into her bag and pulled out her notebook. "Well the first thing on my mind was why is Molly so adamant that these latest bombings have nothing to do with the Irish Republican Army? Why is she so sure? Is she somehow connected to people that may know? I hate to ask her. She has been so nice to us, and I really don't want to upset her. So the first thing on my list was to check today's paper and library archives for recent IRA activity. Maybe one of the geek squad I met the other day will know of an actual IRA member I could interview."

She heard me gasp but ignored me.

"I'm also trying to help you with your land so I added to my list" glancing down at her notes she read, "Check to see what government building would house the country's records. There has to be a way you can save it without costing you an arm and a leg."

"Mary…"

"Okay, this is where it gets interesting. You know when you have the distinct feeling a guy is checking you out? Well I felt that and also felt like I had been zapped with a lightning bolt. I looked around to see who or what was causing it. I spotted this guy looking directly at me. As soon as I looked at him, he quickly began to read the paper. I thought it strange, because if he wanted to catch my attention, why not keep eye contact? I thought maybe he is shy. I ignored him and continued to write. But I couldn't concentrate so I checked him out. He was sitting in the aisle seat across from me, one row back. He has wavy brown hair, shoulder length, wearing this brown leather aviator's jacket, nice and worn. He looked so cool. Like a fashion model. I kept thinking that *there is one Irish souvenir I would love to take home.*"

"Mary your killing me here, so tell me already, did you meet him? Did he ask you out?"

"I will get to it; let me tell you in order. Many folks started to get up for the upcoming stop, and I glanced outside to see that we were at College Green. I packed away my journal and joined the line ready to exit. Just as I made my way a few steps to the aisle, the guy in the jacket stood up and motioned for me to step in front of him in line."

"Well, what did you say?"

"I said thank you, and smiled, noticing that he looked even better up close. He has unusually colored light gray eyes, almost silver but somehow they went perfectly with his strong features. He is built like a runner, all tall and lean, just the way I like them. I hated to leave the bus with Mr. Perfect behind me, but that was my stop.

"I walked through the front gate to the Regent House entrance to the college grounds. I knew just where I wanted to go. You must see this place, I feel so at home there after just one day. I walked around the Campanile to the statue of George Salmon, the college provost from 1888 to 1904. I noticed yesterday that many of the female students patted this statue in passing. I later learned that dear George fought bitterly to keep women out of the college. He carried out his threat to permit them "over his dead body" by promptly dropping dead when the worst came to pass. And of course with the Irish people's great sense of fun, dear George was given a greeting by many of the women he tried so hard to keep out. So of course I smiled up at George and gave him a pat."

We both laughed at that and she continued with her long drawn out story. I knew from experience that one never rushed Mary when she was telling a story or as I liked to say, giving a report.

"I headed to Library Square, passed the Old Library's Long Room, where the line of tourists had already gathered to view the *Book of Kells*. Bridget you must see it."

"I promise I will someday, go on with your story, did you see Mr. Perfect again?"

"I did but don't rush me, I'll get to it. Let's see, I was heading to the library. I just love the library, I'm so thankful to find myself in the same building that houses over three million books. Anyway, as I entered the main foyer, I was greeted by Katie, a fellow geek who works the information desk part-time to help pay the hefty tuition. We had hit it off right away when I asked her for directions to an Internet café yesterday. She told me that one reached Temple Bar by one of the fourteen city bridges. Later we had lunch at Temple Bar's Cyberia Café, where Katie introduced me to her friends and showed me around the area.

"As we walked to the café, Katie told me of the River Liffey. She said that it tis not a notable river, but it meanders through the city and adds to the country charm. James Joyce immortalized the river's spirit as Anna Livia, the woman lying in sculptured form in the middle of O'Connell Street. Of course the Irish call that beautiful art "the floozy in the Jacuzzi." Her friends were also great fun, but it was in the library that I felt completely at home.

"Okay don't give me that face Bridge, I'm getting there. After several hours and armed with a list of contact names and places, I waved good-bye to Katie, headed back over to the café to get a cup of coffee and get on-line. My Web search was frustrating. It looked as if a great deal of what I needed wasn't yet uploaded from hard copies, and I would need to spend the next day at the Hall of Records.

"As I sent an e-mail to David, a fellow techie and friend of Katie's who works at the *Irish Times,* I got that feeling again, I looked around, and there he was. Mr. Perfect was sitting at a table in the back of the café looking directly at me. I shivered and enjoyed the feeling of that energy bolt and wondered at the strange coincidence that brought Mr. Perfect to this café at the same time I was there.

"Funny *coincidence,* did he ask you out, are you seeing him again?"

"Bridget calm down, he is just a guy, now where was I? Oh yeah, David answered my e-mail right away; Katie must have let him know that I would be in touch and what info I was looking for. He had heard that there was an IRA old-timer who often gave interviews and his opinion on current activity. The problem was how to approach him. David had said that he was some high mucky-muck in the Hibernians, but he wasn't available on-line. I guessed I would need to call him to make an appointment and then go to his home in Howth, which my handy-dandy guide said was a village only a short train ride from Dublin.

"I copied down the contact info, thanked David, and signed off. I had to call this IRA guy but I had no phone. I looked over at Mr. Perfect again and smiled. Leaving my book bag to save my table, I walked over to where he was sitting.

"I thought I would take the comic approach, so I said, 'Hi, fancy meeting you ah . . . here'. Bridget, *I stuttered.* What the heck was that? I *never* stutter. I tried again. I managed to say 'Hi, my name is Mary', this time without stuttering, and put out my hand to shake his in greeting. He just looked at me and then looked at my hand, as if he didn't understand what I was offering. It would be just my luck. I thought, Mr. Perfect is mentally challenged.

"Mary...."

"Well he ignored my outstretched hand, what would you think?

"I tried again. I reminded him that we sort of met this morning on the bus but I got no smile, just a blank look you would expect to see on a poker player.

Finally he said, "*Yes.*"

"Great, a man of very few words. So I said, 'Hey, I noticed your cell phone, and I was wondering if I could pay you for a call to Howth'. Bridget, I tell you this guy is so hot, who cares if he is minus a personality. In this case, looks are *everything,* she laughed."

I laughed with her, happy to see her enjoying herself.

"Mr. Perfect's face was deadpan, like no expression *at all,* and he didn't even give me his name. He said, in a cold voice, 'My Mobile? You want to use my mobile? Ah...no need to pay. I will loan you it.' He has a great accent unlike any I'd heard so far. Okay, so he was acting a little strange, not a real Mr. Perfect, but he does have the most beautiful eyes, and the rest of him isn't bad, either.

"He handed me his cell then took it back as if he thought better of it, like I would steal it or something. Then he says, 'It's a wee bit tricky. Let me dial that number for you.'

"Yeah, like because you're blonde, you don't know how to use a cell, is this guy for *real?*"

"That is what I thought, but I needed his phone so I read off the number David gave me. I could've sworn I saw a look of shock on his face, but I couldn't tell for sure since it was gone so fast. He dialed the number and said to whoever answered. 'One moment please there is a young miss here wants to speak with you'. He handed me the phone. When I finished speaking, I closed the cell, thanked him and handed it back."

"I gave him that *I want to hang with you smile* and told him that the man I called sounded great, that I was to meet him right away. I asked him if he knew where the subway is. So he says, '*Subway, oh, do you mean the new sandwich place,' tis only a few streets away*'. I laughed and said, no, I meant the DART station, the Dublin Area Rapid Transit. I told him that I needed to go to the village of Howth. Then he says, '*now, that is a great coincidence, for I am heading that way myself. Do you mind if I ride along with you?*"

"Another coincidence my eye Mary, what's this guy up to? Not that I don't think he is after you for your looks. But what gives, no one is that shy."

"I know, I thought the same thing but he sure is the nicest looking guy I have seen in a long time. Something about him really gets my blood boiling; I really like that tall thin runner body type. So I told him, Sure, let's go. And I finally found out his name, it's Simon."

"Simon?"

"I think it's a family name, his father is English, so he spends time on both sides of the pond, as he calls it, and I just love his accent. After that brief conversation, we walked along in silence to the DART station. I would've recognized it anywhere. It looks like an El station at home. Simon paid the fare for both of us, and we walked through the turnstile and up a large flight of gray concrete steps. I was reaching in my bag for my wallet to pay him back when we reached the top of the stairs, and what I found wasn't the subway I expected, but a clean, open-air station. White subway tile covered the walls, and colorful benches lined the four-city-block-long station. Everything is just as one would expect in a train station, except it was clean. No trash, no graffiti. It was bright and cheerful, just perfect. Simon saw me staring and the most amazing thing happened. He smiled. That smile is brilliant. His whole face softens, and his eyes glow with laughter. I'm not sure how much time passed, but it went by quickly, and neither one of us had said a word. We just stood there staring at each other; if someone looked closely, I bet they would've seen sparks flying.

"The train came and Simon let me lead the way, and I, of course, chose a seat by the window. He sat next to me. The train sits on a raised set of tracks about three stories above street level. From my viewpoint, I could clearly see the classical Georgian architecture for which Dublin is famous. I was again mesmerized by the red-brick houses and the elegance of their doors. Some had a pillar or column on each side, some a side window on either flank, or some had a graceful fan light in the semicircular tympanum above the door. Simon must have noticed my look of rapture, for he leaned over and pointed out the Custom House. He told me that it's among Dublin's greatest public buildings."

Mary paused for a breath and to check her notes, but she was on a roll so I knew that there was no sense in telling her again to hurry up. When she has a report to make or story to tell, she is very detailed. It drove me nuts but there was nothing I could do but sit and listen.

"The Custom House built in 1781, has great detailing, you have got to see it. An Irish sculptor, Edward Smyth, carved the heads over the Custom House arches, each representing an Irish river. Before they went to the euro currency, there was an earlier set of Irish bank notes that bore a drawing of one or the other of those heads. It seems that the higher the value of the bank note, the greater the smile of the head on it!"

"Mary, are you telling me that even the Irish bankers have a great sense of humor?" I laughed. She looked up from her notes and her face was aglow with good memories and excitement.

"It sounds like they do, can you believe it?" we both laughed.

"Bridge, that train ride was so much fun; I could see rooftops, back windows, and sometimes whole streets of homes and gardens. To look at these gardens was to enter a world of wonder away from the hustle and bustle of city life. These small suburban gardens of Eden seemed to be growing more plant varieties than I had ever seen, or read about. I guess it's because of the constant moisture in the air over here.

"I told Simon that it was an Irishman who turned formal gardening on its head in the last century. I asked him if he had read *The Wild Garden* by William Robinson written around 1870. He admitted he hadn't, didn't even try to impress me, *I like that.* Well I told him that in the book Robinson sums up the 'romantic jungle' atmosphere Irish gardeners hope to achieve, voluntarily or otherwise. Before then formal features and artificial effects were very popular, but he stated that they were not always appropriate in an Irish garden setting, where nature tends to reign supreme.

"Simon didn't give me that macho man look like *do I look like a guy that would read a gardening book,* instead he said that he missed that particular book, but the author was correct. His mother always said that no matter how she and others try to impose order and organization on a garden, plants will step in and take over, and do things their own way, not hers or theirs. We both laughed. *Oh Bridge, he has the greatest laugh.*"

"Okay Mary, please tell me *you're going* to see him again."

"We both are, but let me finish."

"It was a great ride. The scenery was spectacular, and for only a couple of Euros, I could see so much more than we could by car. We have to take time to take a few train rides."

"I'm sure we will someday soon." I promised.

"Well Howth station is the last stop on the line. The doors open on one side of the platform, and on the opposite side there were people waiting to take the train back to the city. As we stepped onto the platform, I was amazed to find that flowers had been planted just beyond where the train stopped. Right next to the train tracks!

"You have got to be kidding me?"

"No, I even took some pictures to show you later, I knew you would never believe me," she smiled.

"We walked up a few steps to a sidewalk in a beautiful village. Simon turned left and began walking as I stood still and gasped.

I felt as if I had stepped back in time. The guidebooks said that Howth is a pretty little town, built on steep streets running down to the waterfront. But *pretty* was far from the incredible sight that welcomed me as soon as I left the train station. It was amazing! My senses were on overload. Just glancing around, I could see the village shops in that beautiful weathered brick. Add in castle ruins, an old monastery, and the brilliant color of early spring flowers that were everywhere, and I was at a total loss for words. I looked around and realized that I was standing alone with my mouth wide open. I looked like a total *tourist.*"

"We *are* tourists, so what happened to Simon?"

"I ran to catch up with Simon at the corner. I held onto his arm, and was about to ask for directions to Mr. O'Keefe's house, when I looked beyond him to the ocean. I just stood still and gaped. I must have had that attractive fish look. I had read that Howth was now a major fishing center and yachting harbor, but to read about it and see it were two different things. I knew that my mouth was hanging open, but for the life of me, I couldn't do anything about it. I was standing on a sidewalk that was a block away from the ocean. The scene that greeted me was one straight out of a faeire book. A short distance offshore, I could see Ireland's Eye, a rocky sea bird sanctuary with the ruins of a sixth-century monastery. There is an ancient Martello Tower at the northwest end of the island, and the east end plummets into the sea in a spectacular sheer rock face. There were hundreds of birds around the island, and I could even see seals."

"I can't wait to see it, it sounds magical."

"It is. I caught Simon looking at me, but I didn't let go of his arm. He felt so strong. His gray eyes had gotten darker and he looked as sexy as hell. Bridge, I think he likes me!'

"Of course he likes you, you idiot."

"I asked him if I had died and gone to heaven. It's all so fantastic! 'I so want to go out there'. I managed to say to him while pointing out to sea."

"He said that for a few Euros, Doyle and Son's will take us out to the island, if there are enough folks to make it worth their while. He warned me to not wear shorts if I plan to visit the ruins. They are surrounded by a thicket of stinging nettles."

Mary the scholar was in full swing, and gone was Mary the private eye. I was sure that Sherlock Holmes never was distracted by the scenery, but it sounds like Mary was blown away.

"Mary did you meet the IRA guy?"

"Sure, but wait, I will get to that part. When I turned away from the ocean, I spotted more ruins near the center of the town, and ran toward them and Simon followed me. He told me the ruins were of St. Mary's Abbey. The abbey was founded in 1042. Supposedly by a Viking King!"

"My Gawd this country is really old, isn't it?"

"You could say that. I continued to pump Simon for details, when he finally slowed down to take a breath; I realized that we've been walking straight uphill for the past half hour. I dug in my pocket for the address and looked back down the hill to the village. The view had me again forgetting where I was, and what my plan was."

"Bridget can you believe it, I forgot to ask him if he knew where I could find Mr. O'Keefe's home, his address is just a name 'Bookhaven', When David told me that the house just had a name and not numbers, I thought maybe I would find only a few houses in this village and they would all have signs over the door. Now I realized that I would need a street address to find his home among the hundreds surrounding this large town. I asked to borrow Simon's phone again. He said that there was no need to call. That we were not far, He said that he was familiar with Bookhaven, that it was just a few blocks from where we were standing."

"Hah, another coincidence and you still went with him?" I asked in shock.

"You have to meet him to understand. Anyway Simon pointed up the hill and began walking quickly in that direction. I asked him how he knew the address and if all the homes were given names instead of addresses around here? He said, No, it's just that some of the older homes have names that were bestowed on them a long time ago, and if you are local, you begin to recognize them'."

"Did he mean he was from Howth?"

"That is what I was going to ask but the walk began to get very steep, and I had trouble keeping up with him. We were passing some tall, old stone walls covered in vines. I had a dozen more questions about each of the homes, but before I could get my breath to ask, Simon stopped at the base of a long driveway. He pointed to a three-story, red brick home with two large picture windows on either side of a brightly painted green door. Then he said, 'Well, I will be off, then. Nice visiting with you.' Can you imagine, the idiot, like he was just going to leave me after I thought we had connected, what a jerk?"

"Did you stop him? You didn't go into that house alone, did you?"

"No, I stopped him I grabbed a hold of his arm. I asked him since he knew this guy, then maybe he could come in with me? But Bridge I stammered again, now when have you ever heard me stammering, what gives with that?"

"So maybe you like him or it could be that *you realized you were an idiot* going to interview a known IRA member by yourself! *What's the matter with you?*"

'I really didn't want to admit it, but now that I was there, I was scared. What can I say; you're the one that got me reading all of those Sherlock Holmes books."

"Did he go with you?"

"Sure, but he wasn't very excited about the idea. I found out why later the rat fink. When I think of how I thanked him."

"So go on already."

"We walked to the front door and as I had come to expect in Ireland, there was a shiny brass knocker, on a brightly painted door. But before I could knock, the door was opened by a tall older gentleman. He has a strong, no-nonsense voice, with a heavenly accent. I was stuck dumb; I didn't know what on earth to say. He sure didn't look like what I had expected, but then again I don't know what I had expected. Mr. O'Keefe was in his late sixties, around six-feet tall, and rail thin. Except for the black-rimmed glasses, he would pass for a cowboy in an old western movie. He had that rugged outdoors look. He was all smiles when he greeted me and shook my hand, then he looked past me to Simon and I thought I saw him frown."

"He probably didn't like somebody spoiling his plans to murder you," I said.

"No just wait. I thanked him for taking the time to see us, and introduced Simon. I asked if it was okay if he sat in on our interview. Mr. O'Keefe gave Simon the once over without shaking his hand, then he gestured for us both to come inside. The house was great. The narrow front hallway extended back to another room that looked like a library, but instead of taking us there, he turned right, and brought us to a room that must be the front parlor. In spite of the warm spring day, there was a fire blazing in the beautiful ornate fireplace. Two big, comfortable, brown leather chairs were just calling to have someone come and relax."

"Okay no more home design shows for you," I laughed.

She ignored me and said, "Then it got strange."

"*Then?*"

"Mr. O'Keefe asked me to have a seat and asked Simon to give him a hand with the tea things. Simon set down his book bag and, without removing his jacket, left the room to what I guessed must be the kitchen. I told him that I would be happy to help also and Mr. O'Keefe said that there was no need, and asked me to call him Luke. He said that I must be tired from traveling and asked me to sit before the fire. He took my arm, brought me over to a chair and told me that they would only be a minute."

"So they know each other already?"

"That is what I was thinking but I was so busy trying to put together a list of questions that I didn't give it much thought. Like what do I say? *Oh, by the way, Luke, are you and your cronies responsible for the recent bombings in London?*"

"I would've just stuck to my cover story and gotten out of there."

"Yeah, that's what I planned to do but the only thing I know about the Hibernians is that they march in the St. Patrick's Day parade. I'm really interested in current political issues. I haven't stopped to ask myself why, but who knows, I may decide to move here, and what if it's not safe? The people I met are all great, but they don't appear to be a bit worried about what's happening, and for some reason it's really important to me. I want to find out why Molly thought the IRA innocent of the recent troubles in

England, when the newspaper says they are."

"Go on, what happened next?"

"Luke came back into the room carrying a tray of cookies and placed them on a beautiful, antique, round oak table in the corner of the front parlor. It sat in a nook in front of the large front window. By the stack of papers, he was busy moving to an end table, I guess that it was his preferred spot to work. I felt tension in the air and really looked at him and he looked angry, like he was really upset about something. His forehead was wrinkled and his eyes had darkened, you know that look that that guy Scott at the grocery gets when he is really pissed at his boss?"

"Yeah, I heard he finally quit and went to work at the A&P."

"That's the guy, well Luke looked just like him, and then Simon comes in and looks embarrassed. I didn't know what was going on. Luke gestured me over to the table and pulled out a chair for me. I smiled thanks and found that I was sitting in what must be Luke's chair. When I looked out the window, I could see the front lawn, the street, and down the hill to the ocean. No wonder that was Luke's favorite spot. I would've loved to sit there for hours.

"Luke poured me a cup of tea, which was wonderful. We enjoyed our tea in silence for a few minutes. Then I got up my courage and told them that I had better explain why I was there."

"You didn't tell this guy the truth, did you?"

"What the heck else could I do?"

"Get the heck out of there for one, dummy."

"First, I apologized and said that I came to his home under false pretenses. Then I explained that I wasn't looking for information on the Hibernians. Begged him to believe that what he told me would go no further than that room, told him that I wasn't a reporter, just a nosy person."

"Well, you got that right."

"Alright smarty, I explained why, told them that I'm a research engineer for a computer software company, and my job is to dot the 'I's' and cross the 'T's'. To make sure everything makes sense, and when there are questions, do the research until I find the answers"

"What did he say?"

"Talk about poker faces, I couldn't read what they were thinking so I kept talking. I explained that yesterday I read of a horrible bombing that had taken place in London, and the IRA was blamed by the press. I told them that I spoke with people at the library about it, and they said that the IRA had nothing to do with it and some were very adamant. I also asked people at the Web café, and on the bus. All had the same reaction. I explained that the most outspoken, and positive-sounding person was my friend's Aunt Molly. She sounded as if she just knew that they had nothing to do with this horrific event. I wanted to know—did they?"

"*OhMyGawd*, I can't believe you Mary Margaret, you could've been killed!"

"Well I wasn't, was I? At first they didn't say a word. I looked closely at Luke and Simon, but the only change in expression from Luke was that his left eyebrow rose a bit, but Simon looked in shock. His eyes were as wide as possible, and his mouth had dropped open. Then Luke began to laugh, and if you ever heard the expression "a rusty laugh," then that was it. My question really must have been funny to him, for I could've sworn I could see tears in his eyes."

"He probably agreed with me that you're certifiable."

"I'll ignore that. He finally said, between laughs, 'What in God's blue heaven makes you think that I know anything about the bombings?' I told him that I didn't think he was the bomber. That I knew he was a spokesperson for the IRA. I explained that I had met this really cute guy that liked to hack into the *Irish Times*. When I told him how curious I was, he called a reporter he knew, and I got Luke's phone number. So I knew who he really was. I explained again that all I wanted to know is, if his organization was responsible for the bombings?

"This time there was no laughter, I looked at the change that came over Luke. He sat like a man who had been a soldier, and by the expression in his eyes, had seen the worst. His shoulders straightened. He said, 'Well, Mary, if you are any good at your research, then you know our history and why the IRA was started.' I nodded, and he continued explaining that since peace and prosperity has come to Erie, there is no longer need for violence. There are still a few little loose ends, as he put it that they are working on, but they can be discussed over a pint, not a gun. Then he leaned back in his chair and placed his arms over his stomach. He said that the best way to help me understand was an example from our own country.

"Bridge do you remember when Mom was all upset about a guy called Rodney King?"

"That was a long time ago, something about cops caught on videotape thrashing a black man?"

"Right, well Luke said that the American people didn't lose faith in all of the white officers because of those few rogues. In the past when the IRA was responsible for a crime, they were the first to admit it, and to let the public know why it happened. The Irish people didn't hear from them that they had committed the recent acts and, therefore, they know that the IRA was not olved."

"That makes sense to me, I think."

"Me too, I mean this whole thing is so weird. I asked him why anyone would want the old problems to start up again, why cause anger and hatred. It's almost as if someone is trying to set the seeds to start a war. He said that they were very good questions, and he could guess at their reasons, but never be certain until he found the culprits. He said that there is a long history between England and Ireland, and the time it would take to understand the Irish people and the troubles would take up more than our two-week vacation."

"How did he know we were on a two-week vacation, did he guess?"

"I caught that also, so I asked him, how he knew that I was only here for two weeks. I reminded him that on the phone, I told him that I only had a few more days in the country. He looked over at Simon and had a sheepish look. I guess he realized he had blundered."

"What did he say?"

"Would you like me to heat that up for you?" Mary laughed. "He was stalling for time, so he offered me more tea. When I gave him the look that I was on to his stalling tactics, he said, 'Brilliant. Mary I also enjoy solving puzzles'. It seems that he is currently working on a puzzle, and it involves your land and your solicitor. They believe that she may have been murdered."

"I was hoping that they were wrong," I mumbled.

"What?"

"Nothing Mary, what else did he say?"

"He said that a very good source had informed him that arms

were coming into Knock International Airport. There is a flight daily to and from London, and there is a plane that comes from France once a month. It's the private jet of a major engineering firm. Many of its employees work in Afghanistan. Some of these employees are transported to Ireland for a holiday. They thought it would be simple to catch the folks involved. They searched every vehicle leaving the airport, and every building. They even searched the planes, and found nothing. They would have given up, but their source was the best in the business, and a few days after they received the information, he was found washed ashore, an assassin's bullet between his eyes."

"Who are they?"

"Simon is a British secret agent on loan to Interpol and Luke is a local helping them. They were working the area, when they heard the gossip that a local lady was missing, and that just before she disappeared, she was asking questions regarding land adjacent to the airport. They cannot find her and assume foul play unless they can prove otherwise."

"But why kill Maureen for asking questions about my land?"

""That is what Simon, and all of Interpol has been puzzled with."

"Wow, a secret agent, like James Bond, double 0 7, when do you see him again?"

"I will be seeing a lot of him, and you will also," she smiled that devilish smile.

"Now what have you gotten us into?"

"I asked them to tell me what they had found so far. When they wouldn't tell me, I reminded them that this involved my best friend's lawyer. If she is missing, this might involve your land, and you may also be in danger. So I told them to tell me what they have done, and I would let them know what we plan to do or we could all work together."

"And they went for that? You must be kidding me?"

"Oh they argued with me, said it wasn't possible. Not done. Not ethical to involve civilians, etc. but I let them know that there is no stopping us so it would be best if we teamed up."

"Let me get this straight, the guys from Interpol are thinking that my land may be involved in the shipment of illegal arms into Ireland, and they agree that Maureen's disappearance might not be just a case of a missing woman."

"With what you have just told me, it means he is right. That's why I began to believe that you actually did meet the wee folk. Because we both heard folks talking about Maureen running off with a boyfriend, and no one we have met, while we were together, mentioned murder."

"I so wish they were all wrong."

"Luke has been a soldier since the Stone Age, and if he and Scotland Yard think that there is foul play, then your wee folk must know what's up. They are magical; can't they like wiggle their nose, and put the bad guys behind bars?" Mary asked.

Mick let out a snort, and Mary and I both gave him a dirty look.

"I asked the same thing. Unfortunately, they are not witches like Sabrina and they have this policy not to get involved. They can guide and teach us, if we listen, but this is our realm and we have to fix what's wrong. The only reason they revealed themselves to me was that I have both faerie and leprechaun blood from a long time ago and somehow, God knows how, I'm supposed to help them solve this."

"Do they also think your land is involved?"

"I'm certain, but I don't understand how it could be. It's only forty acres of farmland, and that's mostly bog from what the local real estate agent said. The neighboring farmer wants it just to graze his cattle, so it can't be worth much. The last thing I asked Maureen was to find a cousin, or some family member who could use it, and I think she was researching the family tree . . . so I guess that would be one place to start."

"Well, research is my thing anyway," Mary said, as she hugged me. "Come on, let's keep walking. I'm getting cold, and you need to tell me again what Mick is trying to teach you. Did you say he wanted to teach *you* to think?" She laughed.

I, of course, punched her in the arm as she scampered away with Mick and laughed.

"Mick, me boy, what on earth are you thinking of? You want my friend Bridget to be quiet for a minute, and think clearly? Wow, if you can get that done then you're a miracle doggie."

We continued to laugh, and when we both finally quieted down, we continued to discuss what we needed to do next.

We were laughing again when Molly opened the door. She smiled at us. "I am so glad that you girls had a good time. Did you get a chance to have a good chat and bring each other up to date?"

"Yes, we did," I answered. "I told Mary all that happened in Mayo. Mary is willing to believe me, even though she doesn't believe in faeries. I know that sounds crazy, but as long as it works its okay with me."

"Molly, I was telling Bridget that I met with an old friend of yours today, a Mr. Luke O'Keefe."

"Ah, so you did." Molly said, with a shy little smile as she walked into the kitchen to put the kettle on. She handed us plates.

"Here now, put these things on the table, and we will have a nice long chat, unless you are too tired."

"No, actually we would love to go over our rough plan and get your input," I said, as Mary reached for her pen and notepad.

"Yes, that is good then, isn't it?" Molly said, and began handing us plates piled high with my favorite lemon cream-filled cookies and the teacups. "There, now, where do we begin?"

"Let's make a list of what we know for sure. To start, I think the number-one issue is that Maureen is dead," I said.

"Now, Bridget," Mary said. "How do we know for certain that information is correct?"

"Well, I did sort of speak with her spirit; I would say that that's very clear."

"Well, no offense, Bridget, but I will go and interview the family. Simon would have liked to do that some time ago, when they first heard she was missing, but he couldn't in any official capacity because that would be a warning to whomever the terrorist is."

I looked over at Molly. "I guess that Luke filled you in, Aunt Molly. You know now that they have a missing person, whom they believe is dead, and terrorists off-loading arms at Knock Airport."

"Yes he did, dear. Now there is not much I can do to help you, but I will do whatever I can." Molly said to me then looked over at Mary. "Mary, dear, I am very happy to hear that you and Simon hit it off so well and he will be there to watch over you girls."

I just about choked on my tea. "Okay, Mary, how serious is this with Mr. James Bond? You just said he was a hottie."

"Well, he is a hottie, we're getting off track," Mary said, as her cheeks turned red.

"Okay, number one is finding out what the family thinks happened to Maureen. We can just go and visit with them. They will know that Bridget corresponded with Maureen and may like to meet her. What do you think? Would it work to ask if they have a forwarding address?"

"Great idea Mary, I would love to go with you. Maureen told me so much about her little brothers, and I want to give them the thunder eggs and the Susan B. Anthony dollars I brought for them."

"What is a thunder egg, Bridget?" Molly asked.

"They are great, I will get them to show you." I ran to my bedroom and took out the package I had brought with me and handed it to Molly.

"What's so funny?" I asked a hysterical Molly.

"Ah, Bridget darling, I cannot believe that you brought rocks to Erie," and she continued laughing until tears were rolling down her cheeks.

I was laughing with her since her laughter was contagious, but I was hurt that something I brought so far wasn't appreciated.

"Aunt Molly, these are not just rocks. They have been split open, and you can see how beautiful the insides are. See, the crystal and agate make beautiful images. This one looks like the ocean in a storm," I said, pointing to a particular stone.

Molly picked it up. "You are right, dear. These are beautiful, and I think the boys would love them, but please to sure to point out how special they are inside, because outside they look like any rock you would find in the back yard." She laughed.

"I really hope the boys like them. I didn't know what to get, and I didn't have much money." I ignored the growl I heard from

Mick and continued. "The saleslady at Macy's told me that all boys would love these."

"I'm sure that they will, Bridget" Mary said. "Now please let us get back to the list."

"You are right, sorry. Okay, what should we say is number two?" I asked.

"Well, I would say the next question is why someone would want your land so bad that they would kill over it." Mary said, writing.

"Wait!" I shouted. "Why do you think that my land is the reason someone killed Maureen? That's just crazy, Mary, it's only forty acres of bog. I refuse to believe that a nice young woman could've been killed because of my request to find a relative to take over the land."

"Bridget, until we know more, we must assume that it was your land that was the reason for her death." Mary looked at the stricken look on my face then continued. "But we may find out that she was working on something else. That would be a great task for you. Why not go back to the law firm and see what information you can find out?"

"Okay," I said, feeling a little hopeful. "I will add that to my to-do list. Aunt Molly," I asked, "do you think any of Maureen's neighbors will speak with us about her, and the possibility that she may have run off with a boyfriend?"

"Well, dear, you are a likeable person, and I am sure some may, but let me try and see what I can find out."

"You will come to Mayo with us?" I asked.

"Well, for a day or two to see you both on your way, but I have to return home shortly to cover my obligations," Molly said.

"That is great news, even a couple of days would be

wonderful. Should I call Barbara and see if she has another room available?"

"No, dear, I don't want to intrude on Barbara's business. I will find a room in the village. That way I can walk around and not need to bother you with driving me about."

"Well, Mary, it looks like you have your list. The three of us will attempt to find out where Maureen was last seen, and what she was working on. Should we leave for Mayo tomorrow?" I asked.

"If you don't mind, can we wait until Wednesday?" Mary asked. "I have some more research to do. I wish I had a wireless Internet card so I could get some research done at the bed-and-breakfast and while we're traveling, but they are so expensive."

"I wonder how good the reception is in the country." I asked Mary. "It may not be worth getting."

"It should be very good, Bridget. Ireland is now a technology country; they have Intel, Microsoft, HP, and a dozen other top companies here. I bet those tech guys will make sure it's easy to get wireless anywhere in the country," Mary said.

"Oh, I didn't realize that. Well, let's check the cost—maybe it's cheaper over here. And could we get one before we leave Dublin?"

"Mary, dear, why don't you write down what it is that you will be needing, and I will see if my friends have one lying about," Molly said.

"I don't think what I need will be that common, Molly," Mary explained.

"Hush now. Just write it down and I will see what I can do for you," Molly said, with a grin.

Well, Mary thought, leprechauns were known to be shoemakers in the old stories, and maybe today in the land now called the Celtic Tiger they manufacture computer chips. She smiled and continued her list.

## Chapter 14

# More Questions

"Mary, are you okay back there? I don't think these cars were built for three adults, a laptop, and a dog. Sorry about that."

"I'm doing okay, we will need to stop often to let Mick out, and for me to get some circulation back in my legs," Mary groaned.

We had to postpone our trip west for two days, but what a busy two days. For the first two hours of the trip no one spoke, which I thought had more to do with our all-night brainstorming sessions than the city traffic.

As I dealt with the death-defying Dublin rush-hour traffic, I tried to figure out how we would get this all solved in a few days. No matter what Mick said, I doubted there was any way we could afford to stay longer.

*If we try to stay longer than two weeks, Mary would be on vacation with no pay, and anyway, I need to get another job and . . .*

I heard Mick groan in my head. "When are you going to learn to relax, and know that all of your needs will be met if you just turn them over?"

"Well," I replied silently, "it could be that it's not my habit, and you know that I'm a major worrier. How does anyone do everything that you have been drumming into my head these past few days? Let me see if I have it right. First I need to be still, and not think of anything, and if I do, let it be something from this moment, and something positive. Like how nice this horrible traffic is?"

Again the groan but I ignored it and continued. "Second, I'm to be grateful for all that I have received and will receive in the future. Third, I need to look at any challenges I'm facing and ask for assistance in meeting those challenges . . . or as you say, turn them over to a higher power, right?"

"Yes," Mick replied. "You are a grand listener, but now take what you have learned and put it into action. If something negative comes into your mind like 'Where is the money going to come from?' you can change that *to 'Thank you* for the funds to meet this challenge' and leave it alone. You could start with not thinking of the horrible traffic, and instead try being grateful that you are in Ireland and have the means to hire a car."

"You're right, Mick," I agreed, "I'm sorry to be so grumpy, but you have to admit, this all is a bit overwhelming. I will work harder. I think I really am making some progress. I promise to try my best to let go of worry. You know, I do love this city. The architecture is fantastic, and since the traffic is so slow, I get to enjoy it more. How is that?"

"Ah, now, that is brilliant. Keep up the fine work, lass, you are doing grand."

I was able to keep on the mental track that Mick suggested for the next few minutes, but then my thoughts returned to the issues we were facing.

Through her web café contacts, Mary had met with several Trinity College students. They were in a work-study program, under a grant from America's Intel computer company. Mary explained to them that we hadn't been able to find anything on-line regarding the property in Garnaqugoue, even in a public records search.

They explained to her that all records are kept in Dublin at the Hall of Records, and on the original paper—they weren't part of any local or public on-line record. That wasn't all that unusual. It was really expensive to go back through decades of data and digitally scan them into a database. Usually only the larger, wealthier countries could afford to do that.

Places like Ireland would rather focus on putting their Euros to better use, but thanks to the grant, these students had been given the monumental task of getting the ancient Hall of Records and National Archives files computerized.

Mary had asked them if they would dig deep for any records with the name of Garnaqugoue or Carin, and they did.

Since the students were the first to be given the task of computerizing Ireland's record, they had started with the earliest recordings. They had uncovered hundreds of ancient wooden boxes with scrolls rolled up and tied with faded ribbons and were anxious to record these right away.

What they found was a grant of land to the Carin family for services rendered to King Henry II and Pope Aidan, which was later upheld by the Republic of Ireland. Their findings were even more unbelievable than meeting a leprechaun.

When she finished meeting with the students, Mary announced that we were now looking at not one, but many possible suspects. I think we were all worn out from trying to make sense of all this.

Even though I found driving the country roads relaxing, I was ready to get back to work.

*There might be something in what Mick keeps nagging me about. I have been working on stopping the non-stop jibber-jabber going on in my head, and just being in the moment, as he explained, and I feel a little more relaxed. I won't be telling him anytime soon; he has an overgrown ego already,* I thought.

Just then I heard a doggie snort and realized that he must have been monitoring my thoughts. The rat fink!

"Okay, you guys, are we ready to review the notes we made last night?" I asked.

"You mean this morning," Mary groaned.

"Of course dear, Mary, if you have your copy handy, could you read it again?" Molly asked.

Mary powered up her laptop, and typed quickly on the keyboard. "Okay, here goes: Item One: Land Grant. Attached is a copy of what appears to be the original deed for the Carin family's land, and the deed states that the land owned by Bridget is actually four hundred hectares, not forty hectares as she was originally informed by the solicitors and local agent.

"Research to date: We met with Deidre, a renowned real estate agent and Molly's daughter-in-law, therefore trustworthy. She confirmed that the deed was official. Deidre provided us with a list of the current residents who have been living and working the land since 1902.

"The families who have lived and worked on the land for three generations but don't have a land deed are: Martin Finnegan, sixty hectares; Sean Brennan, sixty hectares; Tom Lydon, forty hectares; Luke Snee, forty hectares; and Patrick Gallagher, sixty hectares.

"Further research shows that the Snees, Brennans, Lydons, and Gallaghers have intermarried over the years and they now have one farm of two hundred hectares.

"First possible suspect is current owner of Killkeary Farm, Tom Brennan age sixty-four. His home is located only a mile from the airport. Our second possible suspect is Martin Finnegan, age sixty-nine. His home is located on the north side of the school.

"The missing one hundred hectares is now called Knock International Airport. That leaves Peter Carin with the forty hectares that the lawyers claim is the only land currently owned by Bridget's family.

"Question: Are current residents aware that they don't own their land? The solicitor's office says that the land is only forty hectares and not worth very much. Also, when we called and spoke with them about this new deed, they said that the deed we have is false. If we were to bring this new deed to court, they predict close to a million Euros in legal fees and many years of battle.

"Question: Why don't they even want to see the deed we have found?

"A Galway agent was hired by the solicitors to research the land, and he reported that it was bog land worth only twenty thousand Euros. The one and only real estate agent in town said he has a buyer for the forty hectares who is willing to pay twice what the agent from Galway estimated the land to be worth. We later found that prospective buyer is the current tenant who is still trying in court to get the land for free."

Mary stopped her reading. "Okay, I have another question to add to our list. Why would the tenant be willing to pay double the amount the agent says the land is worth when the solicitor says he has a good chance of winning his claim and getting the land for free?"

"Perhaps to keep the issue out of court," Molly suggested.

"You may be right," Mary said, and continued reading. "Part of the family land grant includes Knock International Airport. The story that everyone has heard was that the area priest would travel by mule to visit the elderly farmer who had worked the land since childhood. The patch of land he traveled was smooth and flat, and consisted of one hundred hectares.

"When the farmer passed away, it was reported that he gave the land to the church. The priest saw the potential for the airport and gave the land to the county for that purpose only.

"Question: Could the dying farmer have confessed the real owner of the land and the church didn't want to get involved?

"We all know the church; it's not like them to give away valuable land. I heard that the local people were very surprised when an international airport was built, since Shannon International Airport is only a couple of hours away in County Clare, and it's the second largest airport in the country. Knock is a seldom-used airport with only one daily flight to London" I don't understand that one at all. Sorry, Mary, go ahead, what else do you have?"

"Just one last question: Why was it built? Wouldn't the county officials have had to research the ownership? Did the priest discover that the land wasn't owned by the farmer, so the church couldn't legally accept it?"

"No wonder we're all tired; we have done a great deal so far. But all we have is more questions. We sure have our hands full," I said.

"But that's not all of the mystery. When I was researching County Mayo and Garnaqugoue, I found a document, which is a decree, or patent, from Queen Elizabeth. It seems that Elizabeth I had set her heart upon the colonization of Mayo by English Protestants.

"I have some notes of the official history of this area. It's long, but please bear with me. I think it's very interesting. In this document I found, it says that Elizabeth I, sent Sir John Popmish, her attorney general, to 'coax the gentry in several districts to send over the junior members of their families as undertakers.' I guess that's the old way of saying *caretakers*," Mary said, and continued reading. "She 'caused letters to be written to people of distinction in every shire in England with the same intent.'

"To 'such as would come, she offered estates at a fee of only twopence and threepence an acre. For every twelve thousand acres thus bestowed, the undertaker was to plant eighty-six English Protestant families upon the land, and smaller or larger grants were to be peopled in the same ratio. Bogs and mountains were to pay no rent until improved, and were then only to be charged at the rate of a halfpenny an acre.

"Now this is the part that's very, *very, interesting* to me. The planters were to be English, and their heirs were to marry no one but those of *English* birth. The settlers were not to permit any of the *mere Irish* to be maintained in any of their families. Every freeholder, from the year 1590, was to be English.

"Do you see why I'm puzzled?" Mary asked.

"Sure, I do. I don't think there are many, if *any*, English Protestant families in the area. What do you think, Molly?"

"I think you are right, Bridget. Elizabeth must have had a change of heart. She was known to be a friend of a certain Grace O'Malley. Perhaps she listened to her and that did not get into your history books.

"Who?" Mary asked.

"Don't worry about the past Mary, it looks as if ye have your hands full with the current challenges, I'd say," Molly said smiling.

"Any suggestions on where we start?" I asked.

"I'm brain-dead right now, Bridge. I need to think this all over and see if I can make sense of it," Mary replied.

"I am with you, dear. I am also at a loss," said Molly.

"Well," I suggested, "why don't we stick with the original plan? I will see what I can get from the tenant, real estate agent, and the solicitor. Mary will interview the families currently on the four hundred hectares. Molly, please go ahead with your plan of speaking with the town gossips. We need to find out as much information as we can about all the suspects and any stories of Maureen."

Mary and Molly agreed to the plan and were silent during the rest of our drive to Mayo.

We dropped Molly off at a three-story, brick-front home in the village of Ballina. It was an older home, and a little shabby looking, but it did have a bright-green front door with a 'Room for Let' sign in the front window.

"Are you sure you want to stay here by yourself, Aunt Molly?" I asked.

"Sure I am. Haven't I stayed here before? I will be fine. I will meet you tonight at 8:00 p.m. at the pub; we can have a bite to eat and a chat."

With that, she grabbed her overnight bag and walked to the front door. We waited until an older woman opened the door, took one look at Molly, greeted her with a large smile and a hug, took her bag, and ushered her inside.

"Well, I guess we're all set until tonight. Where should we start?" I asked Mary and Mick. When I got no answer, I suggested, "I think we really need to meet Maureen's family. Let's drop our bags at the B&B. I'm sure we can use Barbara's phone book to gather up all of the numbers we will need."

"It has come to my attention that you are not pleased that my spirit takes shelter at your ancestral home. That you believe you no longer owe me a debt. Is that correct My Lord?"

"A thousand pardons, My Lady. Of course, you are always welcome at Howth Castle. I just asked a banshee or two for more appropriate lodgings. I thought that you might be more comfortable, say, in Dublin, where there is much more going on these days," Mick said, with head bowed as he knelt at her feet.

He could hear Padraig silently whisper, "not wise, me bucko, I would stay kneeling if I were in your place right now."

The queen that Grace was became evident as she looked down at Mick from her throne chair that he returned to her from one of his many quests. The deeply carved lions' heads with bared teeth, the ornate heraldic eagles, the exquisite scrollwork and cushions upholstered in a fine tapestry, shook as her anger increased.

"Lord Howth, the comment I heard was that you thought it was time I moved on as you or your family no longer owe me a debt . . ." She stood to emphasize her words, and in a tone that many have learned to fear, she said, "Need I remind you that I was once loved by all mortals as the Queen of Ireland and by the immortals as the Queen of all the Faeries?"

Now I am in for it, Mick thought, I will be here for hours as she relives her days of past glory.

# Chapter 15
## The Search Begins

W e followed the directions that Mrs. O'Hara had given us and stopped in front of a large brick two story farm home. The yard was a beautiful variety of elegant landscape, flowers and toys. I would've stayed in the car longer, hoping to postpone the dreaded interview, but the front door opened and three young boys, ages five to ten came running to greet us. They politely asked questions as they accompanied us to the front door. "Did you come all the way here from the United States? Did you fly on one of those big planes? Can I play with your dog?"

We laughed as we tried to answer their questions and then Mick got up on his hind legs and did a little dance for them and they were all giggles.

"A thousand welcomes, you must be Bridget and Mary, come in please and make yourself at home."

We were still smiling at Mick's antics when we turned to meet the woman with the gentle voice that greeted us. I hope the shock didn't show on my face as I shook Mrs. O'Hara's skeletal hand. She looked as if she weighed ninety pounds soaking wet. She had dark black hair shot through with a great deal of gray. I don't think she was very old but her face was a mass of deep set wrinkles. The black shadows under her eyes added to the picture of a woman on the edge.

Mrs. O'Hara showed us into a large warm kitchen with a beautiful round wooden table that was set for four. "I hope you will have a bite. This is my daughter Patty, sit down now and we will have a nice chat."

We shook hands with a woman around our age wearing nice brown slacks and a sweater-set. "Hi," she said. "This won't take but a moment, sit down Mam, I will get the things." Patty turned towards the pantry and Mary went to help her.

"You have a wonderful home Mrs. O'Hara, thank you for meeting with us."

"We feel we know you already, or maybe I shouldn't have said that. You see Maureen loved emailing you and she told us of your holiday to the Wild West. We all had a great laugh over the postcard you sent. I am afraid that the boys will hound you with questions."

"They are great kids; I brought them something from Montana that I thought they might like, is it okay to give it to them?"

Her beautiful dark blue eyes watered up and I was afraid that she would cry but she said, "My Maureen told us that you were a caring woman. I wish she was here to greet you herself." She paused and I watched as she straighten her freshly starched apron over her thin cotton housedress, pull her thin shoulders back and take a deep breath to help her gain control over the tears that threatened. I almost lost it myself but luckily the boys and Mick came in to join us.

"They are a nice family." I said, as we got back into the car.

"I almost slipped up and told them that we would find her murderer, but dear God, we have to find her body soon! Did you see her mother? She looks as if she already knows something is horribly wrong and has not been able to sleep for weeks."

"I agree. It was a good thing you came along; I was able to speak with her older sister while you were with the rest of the family."

"Yes, that worked out well. No matter what Molly thought, I think that the boys did like the thunder eggs, don't you?"

"Well, I'm not sure it was the rocks as much as your stories of cowboys and Indians. Like, when have *you* ever met a real Indian?" Mary laughed.

I ignored her question. "What did you find out from her sister?"

"You were right, Bridge. Patty said that Maureen was doing research into the Carin family and the Garnaqugoue property. It was being talked about in town that you wanted to find a relative to take over the land. They all thought you were some rich Yank who didn't need to be bothered with an Irish farm."

"Oh, no, I didn't think of that. I guess the folks around here don't know of any poor Yanks. I did tell her that I had no money even to make the trip over here, let alone the money to keep the farm going. She must have kept that bit of news to herself. "Do you think Maureen found out about the original land grant, which showed I was the owner of the four hundred hectares?"

"I don't think so. I think if she did, she would've said something to her family. No, she was just trying to find one of your local cousins, and perhaps asked one too many questions."

"I wonder why she didn't ask Barbara and her husband to take over the land." I asked.

"Now that's the funny part. Patty said that she did, and they didn't want anything to do with it."

"But that's crazy! We know that Barbara is a smart business-woman. How could she not want land?"

"Well, I guess we had better ask her . . . because Patty said they were the last people she knew that Maureen spoke with."

"Oh my Gawd, Mary, I really like Barbara and her family, heck, they are cousins of mine. Could they really be suspects?"

We had arrived at the pub, and we both just sat there in our car, not wanting to move.

"Come on. This is where Molly said to meet her, and I will buy you a Guinness," Mary said, and gave me a one-arm hug before she grabbed her backpack and jumped out of the car.

I must have looked as sad and confused as I felt, because Mary took my arm and led me into the pub. Just like in the movies, it had a casual and relaxed atmosphere. There were a dozen or so people having lively conversations while enjoying dinner, a drink, or both.

The pub looked at least a hundred years old. The beautiful, dark wood tables and chairs matched the wainscoting. The white paint on the ceiling, and top part of the walls, was tinted yellow from the smoke of sweet-smelling pipes, and one or two ciga-rettes. There were sconces every few feet that gave off a soft light that stopped it from being a dark and dreary place. There were three sections in this very long, narrow room.

The front section had small tables alongside the wall to seat two to four people. The middle section showcased a long bar with gleaming wood polished to a mirror shine that was reflected in the twenty-foot mirror behind it. In front of the bar were old-fashioned brass stools with red leather cushioned seats.

The third section looked as if it was the official restaurant section, having large wooden tables that could seat four to twelve people. That's where we found Molly. She was speaking with a lady in her forties who was wearing an apron. They stopped speaking as we pulled up our chairs.

"Girls, I would like you to meet Sarah. She owns the pub. It has been in her family for several generations. Isn't it a grand place?"

I noticed that Sarah now acted a little standoffish, where before, as we were walking up to them, she was smiling and laughing with Molly.

I smiled. "Hi Sarah, nice to meet you, this is a beautiful place you have here. How old is it? I thought that it might be at least a hundred years old."

Sarah laughed. "Well now, you are right there, it's a least a hundred years old." She turned and winked at Molly. "Have a seat and I will get you a pint, will I?"

Mary said, "I would love a Guinness. What about you, Bridge?"

"I would love a cup of tea, please."

We pulled out a couple of chairs and joined Molly at the table.

"What was that wink about, Molly?" I asked.

"Well, dear, most of the town, including this establishment, dates back to the fifteenth century, so you were right, 'tis over a hundred years old," Molly said, with a smile.

"I keep forgetting that Ireland is centuries old, compared to our mere two hundred years." I looked around for the menu, and Mary pointed to the wall. I read the two items listed and was puzzled.

"We're starving. What would you recommend for dinner, Molly?" I asked, but before she had a chance to answer, a more relaxed Sarah came over with our beverages. She told us of the daily special or carvery. The carvery was the main meat that they would carve for our dinner. We had a choice of the item being carved, or one other that Molly later told us was made with the leftovers from the day before. Today it was ham, and we all agreed that sounded wonderful.

As Sarah left with our food orders, Molly asked if we had made any progress. We explained our visit with Maureen's family, and the calls we had made, setting up appointments for the next day. We were all quiet while we ate the wonderful food. Again we had fresh vegetables, home-baked bread, and two types of potatoes.

"I think we had better walk around the village before we head back. I'm so full I could burst," I said, as Sarah handed Molly the bill.

"No you don't," I said. "You fed us in Dublin. I will take care of that," and I grabbed the bill. I was surprised to notice a sour look from both Molly and Sarah. *Now what the heck did I do wrong? I thought. Will I ever get the subtle nuances of how one should act over here?*

We decided to walk Molly to the room she was renting, which was only four blocks away. The village was picturesque, but the streets were an accident waiting to happen. They were very dark and narrow, and the concrete sections were all uneven. I almost tripped a few times, when I looked up instead of watching each step.

"It looks as if this village could use some money," I commented when Molly grabbed my arm to stop me from falling.

"That is so. It is this way all over Ireland, but I hope things will get better soon," she said, optimistically. "Things are a little worse for wear in this town that's for sure. I wonder why it's so bad."

Mary told Molly about Barbara and her family being approached by Maureen just before she disappeared. We wondered why Barbara had not mentioned it, or even why they didn't say they would take over the land.

"I thought I would ask her tomorrow after breakfast," I said.

"No, dear, please hold off on your questions for now. If they didn't want your land, they may have had a private reason or were scared off by people who will kill to have it. Either way, you would embarrass them with your questions. Yes, it is better to say nothing right now," Molly advised.

We dropped Molly at her door and waited for her to use her key to let herself in. Mary and I joined arms to help each other maneuver the crooked sidewalks. We finally gave up and walked in the street. It turned out that the middle of the street had very safe cobblestones rather than concrete, or the tar we were used to. We were also surprised that there wasn't a car in sight.

"Mary, can you believe this? It's just after ten o'clock, and the town has closed up for the night. There are very few lights in the homes and no traffic at all. Wow, what a change from Brooklyn," I commented.

Mary didn't say anything, and I realized that she had not said much for most of the night. I looked at her as we passed under a streetlight, and noticed a familiar look. Mary was in research mode. She would input data and look at the facts from all angles. While she was in this mental mode, it was best just to be quiet and wait.

We walked back to the car in silence. As we approached, I clearly heard Mick demand to be let out. "Well, it is about bloody time, don't you think? Let me out of this bloody car now."

"Oh, Mick, I'm so sorry. I totally forgot about you. We should have taken you for a walk," I said, silently as I unlocked the door and a flash of white and brown flew by us to find the nearest tree.

"You think? Just because I was sleeping while you enjoyed dinner, you had no reason to leave me in here. The car was parked directly in front of the pub so there was no way . . ." he stopped abruptly.

"No way to do what?" I asked as I looked over to the tree Mick was quickly sniffing.

"A little privacy, if you please," he said, but he didn't answer my question.

I smiled at his very human comment and turned to Mary. "Do you think Mick will be okay in the car all night? Will he be warm enough?"

"Huh? Oh, Mick? Sure he will be," she answered.

I drove a relieved Mick and distracted Mary back to the bed-and-breakfast. I left the window open so that if Mick had a call of nature, he could just jump out and back in. I had made a bed out of a long overcoat that I had brought with me but found no need to wear with the mild weather we were enjoying.

I provided him with a bowl of fresh water and leftovers from our pub dinner. "Will that be okay, Mick? Do you need anything else? I'm sorry you can't come in, but Barbara's daughter is allergic to dogs."

"No, thank you, this will be grand. Thanks for leaving the window open, I like the fresh air," he said, with what sounded like a smile in his voice.

# Chapter 16
## Mary Investigates

The next morning, after a breakfast of cold cereal, toast, eggs, sausage, fried tomatoes, and tea, we headed out. Mary was in research mode and with notebook and pencil in hand she made herself a map of the countryside.

"Are you sure about this?" I asked anxiously.

"Don't worry, Bridge. You know that I know how to drive, I just choose not to. Here they only have minimal traffic, sheep and cows. There is really not a major traffic problem, is there? So stop being a mother hen. I'm just driving to the farms surrounding your land. Get going and tackle the locals and I will meet you at the pub at noon."

"Okay," I said, and got out of the car. Seeing Mick getting ready to join me, I asked, "Are you okay with Mick staying in the car? It would be hard to tie him up outside the offices, and he doesn't have any tags on him in case he got lost."

"No problem, Bridge. Welcome to the ride of your life, Mick," Mary said laughing.

*"Hey, you did not ask if it was okay with me to ride with Mary,"*

screamed an outraged Mick. I ignored him. I waved good-bye as Mary dropped me off in front of the real estate agent's, a few doors down from the solicitor's office.

An excited Molly met with Mary and me for lunch. Molly suggested we get our lunch to go and have a picnic and a nice chat.

"Simon is in town now and he will be joining us," Mary announced.

"That is grand," Molly said, handing Mary her cell. "Please ring him up and tell him to meet up with us at the base of the Reek."

"What's the Reek?" Mary asked, and I was stunned.

"Mary, I thought you devoured those guidebooks. If you don't know of it, then we must go there." I laughed.

"Ah, now, sorry lass; you may know of it as Croagh Patrick," Molly said.

Mary turned to me triumphantly. "Well, even *you* know of Croagh Patrick. It's from the top of that mountain that St. Patrick performed his snake expulsion act, and all of Ireland has been free of venomous serpents ever since."

I stuck my tongue out at Mary and turned to Molly. "Sounds good to me, it would be nice to have a picnic and relax before I meet up with the solicitor later on this afternoon."

Mary called Simon. I paid for our picnic lunch, and Molly collected a shopping bag on wheels that she had packed full of the extras we would need to make our picnic complete.

"It is a bit of a drive to Westport, but one that any visitor to this county must see," Molly said, as she directed me to the correct road. "It is really a shame that you are so busy with this bit of a problem about the land and don't have time to be a tourist, so I thought that we could spend a few minutes each day looking around."

As we passed a sign for Knock, Molly proudly told us the history of this once undistinguished village that has been famous, for over a century, as a site of visions and miracles.

"There is a Basilica of Our Lady, Queen of Ireland, which can accommodate twelve thousand people and was visited by Pope Paul VI in 1974, Pope John Paul II in 1979, and Mother Teresa in 1993," she told us in a hushed, reverent tone."

When we passed another small, discreet sign to a village called Louisburgh, Molly laughed at something Mick must have silently said to her.

"Well, now, our friend Mick says that I am to tell you of another Queen of Ireland, Gráinne O'Malley, or, as you would say, Grace. Every Irishwomen loves the story of Grace and we learn her history by rote. She was a daughter of a Connaught chief who established her own fleet and commanded her own army. From her Clare Island base, she attacked ships of those who had submitted to the English. In 1566, she married Richard Burke, since her first husband had died years earlier. Richard was a neighboring clan chief, and her power grew to such an extent that the merchants of Galway pleaded with the English governor to do something about her.

"In 1574, her castle was besieged, but she turned the siege to a rout and sent the English packing. In 1577, she was held in prison but mysteriously managed to get herself released on a promise of good behavior. Over the next few years, she craftily entered a number of alliances both with and against the English.

"In 1593, she traveled to London and was granted a pardon after meeting Elizabeth I, who offered to make her a countess. She declined. For she already considered herself the Queen of all Ireland."

We all laughed, and Mary continued the story where Molly had left off.

"There is more," she said. "I loved reading about her also. Back in Ireland, she appeared to be working for the English, but the final recorded reference to her was in the English State Papers of 1681. It makes it seem likely that even at her advanced age she was still fiercely independent. An English captain tells of meeting one of her pirate ships, captained by one of her sons, on its way to plunder a merchant ship. By that time, she was more than fifty years of age and for 1681, that was ancient."

Wanting to continue our happy mood, I belted out an old Helen Reddy classic Mary's Mom would sing, "I am woman hear me roar . . ." When Mary and even Molly joined in, I could hear Mick groan. Mary said that he had his head down on the seat, and his paws were covering his ears, which set us in another round of laughter.

"I admire the strong Irish women of our family, and now I understand from where they pull their strength. With such great examples of a spiritual Queen and a Pirate Queen like those two, one has a lot to live up to." I laughed.

"I love reading about Grace." Mary said. "There are so many great stories; she was a very interesting character... I read that in 1574 Grace dropped by Howth Castle on her way back from visiting with Queen Elizabeth I. The Earl of Howth sent a servant to inform her that they were busy having dinner, and refused her entry. Unknown to the Earl his son had been taking a stroll around the gardens with a beautiful young lady when an angry Grace had him kidnapped. To get him returned to his family, his father had to promise that the doors of Howth Castle would always be open to Grace and anyone seeking food and shelter."

"She sounds just like someone I would love to meet." Mary and I laughed but Molly and Mick were very quiet.

⸻⚬⸻

We parked at Campbell's Pub in the village of Murrisk and walked a short way to the picnic area at the base of the mountain. Molly dug into her bag of goodies as Mick ran free over the hillside. Molly pulled out a tablecloth, plates, napkins, and a large tin of biscuits for dessert.

I laughed. "All we're missing now is the tea," and with that I heard a strong male voice call out...

"Well, it looks like I picked up just the right thing to contribute to our feast."

Mary jumped up from her seat at the picnic table and ran to greet a tall, very good looking young man and help him with his burden of two paper cup carriers.

"Aunt Molly, Bridget, I would like to introduce you to Simon," said a beaming Mary.

We smiled and shook hands, but I noticed that Mick was standing very stiff legged and was sizing up our guest.

*"Well, Mick, what's the verdict? Do you think he is okay for our Mary?"*

*"We will see now, won't we?"*

We all dug into our lunch of roast beef sandwiches with a lightly sweetened horseradish sauce that had Arby's beat hands down. When we finished, Mary proceeded to bring us up to date on her morning interviews.

Holding her notes to make sure she reported all of the key points, Mary told us all about her first stop at Killkeary Farm, checking on Mr. Brennan.

"It's a large, two hundred hectare spread, which includes a large farm and what looks like a major housing development that's partially under construction. The homes being built must be the most expensive in all of Mayo. I will do more research on that, but according to the sign posted out front, they are 98 percent pre-sold. There are a dozen or more homes in the area of the main house, and I'm assuming they are for the rest of the family. This so-called farm is set behind a high stone wall and electronically controlled gates.

"There is a small cottage just inside the gate, and as we drove up the drive, we must have triggered something, because this guy opened the gate and asked me my name. After I told him he said that I was expected and came to the passenger side of the car and got in.

"Of course, Mick growled at him, but he ignored Mick and was all business. He introduced himself as Barry Cowan, Mr. Brennan's estate agent. He directed me to continue up the drive and pull to the back of the house to park. I can tell you, our rented little Fiat looked really out of place next to those fancy sports cars. Barry said that Mick should remain in the car, and we walked to the back door.

"The cars were a shock, but this house was something else. This three-story brick home had a very old-world, country-palace look. I oohed and aahed about the house, and finally Barry broke a little smile and started telling me all about it. 'Not many people

can boast that their kitchen doubles as a ballroom,' he said, pointing to the super-size room as we passed it. 'But this beauty can
take eighty for supper, with dancing to follow. The house itself
has eight bedrooms and even includes a twenty-four-foot wine
cellar, accessed from a lift in the conservatory.'

"As he pointed to the right, I could see a two-story, all glass
building attached to the house. We continued into the house, and
as we passed a door he paused and asked if I would like to see a
bit.

"I nodded, as I was actually staring with my mouth open and
unable to utter a word. Barry smiled and told me about the room
I was looking at. He said, 'This marble-trimmed kitchen has eight
dishwashers and twin Agas.'

"What on earth is an *Aga?*" I asked.

"I don't know, I made a note to Google it, but I think he was
referring to the stove. You guys *got to* see this place, you won't
believe it! The kitchen was to die for, opulent and fantastically
well-organized. Barry said that elsewhere on the ground floor is
the utility room, and a 'snug television room', with paneled walls
and surround sound."

"Sounds like a multi-millionaire's house to me," I said.

"A wee bit over the top" Molly agreed.

Mary was no longer looking at her notes as she told us about
the home. She was so excited, her face and eyes were glowing.
She looked so happy. I looked over at Simon, and noticed that
I wasn't the only one enjoying the report and the excitement of
the reporter.

"Then Barry showed me into a library that was a dream
come true. When I told him how much I loved it, he showed
me the mahogany fittings that he said came from a famous hotel

in Scotland. The room was covered in shelving that held books from floor to ceiling on three sides. The window overlooked a garden, which was incredible. I spotted another small cottage, somewhat hidden, at one end of the garden, and he explained that that was home to a couple who clean and take care of the property and they even employ a full-time gardener.

"I agreed that a lot of staff must be needed to keep this home in pristine state. But he said that the working conditions are nothing short of splendid—the utility room, I think that is his way of saying bathrooms, is decorated in French château style with floor-to-ceiling hand-painted units, marble worktops, and a chandelier—one of twenty throughout the house. He then excused himself and went to get Mr. Brennan. I told him that he could take his time because I could spend days in any library.

"After he left, I went over to the bookcase closest to the large mahogany desk to see what books Mr. Brennan read. I was disappointed to find that the walls lined in leather bound books, were in fact just elaborate storage files. I had one of these phony books in my hand when in walked the master himself."

Mary again referred to her notes and continued reporting. "Mr. Brennan is of medium height; I would say about five foot seven, and looks like an old-time boxer. His nose looks as if it had been broken in one too many fights. He has the telltale sign of a heavy drinker, you know, the large red broken veins. He has thick, wavy black hair, with just a touch of gray. He wore very thick, heavy black-rimmed glasses, and had a very white complexion, as if he does not spend much time outdoors. He had a no-nonsense attitude that would go well in any company board room.

"After I thanked him for seeing me and threw out many compliments about his home, he seemed to become a little more at ease. We talked about what I have seen in Dublin, where we're staying, etcetera. Then I realized that *I* was being interviewed, and not the other way around. I quickly explained that I was trying to find out what really happened to Maureen. He ceased the friendly, Irish-host persona. I got short, one-word answers after that."

Referring to her notes she read, "Did you meet with Maureen the week of . . .?" Response: A loud, 'No!' I thought it was interesting that he gave me a no answer before I had a chance to give him a date. Then I asked, "Have you seen Maureen since that date?" ...Response: 'No'. "Do you have any reason to believe that Maureen met with foul play?" Response, 'What are you blathering on about? 'Tis well known that Maureen ran off with someone. She is probably living it up in Dublin. The interview is over; I have more important things to do than gossip with the likes of you.'

"My overall impression is that that family has a lot of money and is in the process of making a great deal more. I would hate to be the person who stood in the way of his money. He should go to the top of our list."

"It sure sounds that way to me." I said looking around the table, and Molly nodded in agreement. Mick looked attentive, and Simon looked analytical.

"My second meeting of the day went very well. I met with Martin Finnegan. When I asked for directions to his place, I learned a lot about him. Everyone loves 'Old Martin.' He goes to church every Sunday and Wednesday. 'Took care of his mother every day of her life' was the story I heard from his neighbor. She only passed away a few years ago, at the great age of ninety-four. The whole town turned out for her funeral. I was also told by the neighbor that the Finnegan family has lived and worked on the same plot of land 'since recorded time.'

"When Martin opened his front door, I knew right away why he is so loved. He looks a little like Santa Claus: a little heavyset, and has a great smile. He is a charmer; I fell in love with him right away. I loved hearing him talk about this part of Ireland. He said that this is probably the part with the richest remains of Celtic ancestors.

"He spoke in some of the old Celtic language and told me a number of legends and faerie tales of the area. He spoke of Ceis Churainn and of Cormac MacAirt, a famous King of Ireland who was reputedly born and raised by a she-wolf. I spent several hours with him, and I really wanted to stay longer. He has a small, two bedroom cozy little cottage, with a large fireplace, I felt very comfortable. I loved hearing his stories. Martin was in a walking mood, so we walked over the hill to your farm, and then just past it to a road directly across from the mystery road where we found the burial mound."

"I don't remember any other road?" I said.

"How on earth we missed seeing it when we were there, I don't know. We were a little preoccupied with the mound.

"We didn't go too far down that road when something strange happened. Martin had been telling me stories of the area, and funny things that tourists have asked him over the years, when all of a sudden he stopped, and said, pointing off to the right, 'Up around that bend there are the turf fields belonging to the Carin family.'

"You got to be kidding me, I own turf fields?"

"He says you do. I also asked him what turf was exactly. I wanted to hear what the folks using it thought it was compared to the dictionaries scientific terms. He said, 'Turf is 100 percent organic peat, it's environmentally friendly. It helps prevent chimney fires, and causes no heavy creosote buildup. Lasts for hours, and there are no sparks or crackles to burn you, the furniture, or the dog!' I told you he was a kick.

"Then he told me of a group in County Clare making a killing selling sod to tourists. We had a great laugh at the outrageous prices they were getting. Everything was fine until I told him that I would love to see the turf field. We continued walking in that direction, and then I asked him if he was sure that the fields belonged to the Carin family. I pointed out that that area is not on your property, and he got really rattled. He said, 'Well, now, let's go back. I am too old to be doing all of this walking anymore.' Then he abruptly turned around, and we headed back to his cottage. After awhile, he started with his funny stories again, but it just wasn't the same," Mary said, as she closed her notebook.

"I think you are beautiful, ah, I mean brilliant . . . ah . . . that is a brilliant report," Simon said.

"I love it, yes, brilliant report Mary, that tells us a great deal," said Molly.

I looked over at Mary. "Great job that's a great deal of work you did. I know we have a lot to talk about, but darn, I have an appointment to talk with the family solicitor now. I can drive Molly back, but why don't you and Simon ride back together," I winked at Mary while Simon wasn't looking. "You can talk over the fine points of our plan and get his feedback. We will meet up later at the pub. What do you think?"

"That is brilliant, Bridget!" Simon said, as he jumped to his feet.

Interlude

Grace was in full stride now, her hands placed behind her back, pacing back and forth across the floor, as she continued her tirade in an ever increasing volume. "If not for that lowly excuse of a cousin, I would still be alive and Queen. As it is now, I can only occupy places I have been before and you dare to want me to leave Howth Castle."

Could clouds come inside? I swear it is getting darker in here, Mick thought as he began to shiver. The air surrounding him became still and his vision blurred. He could feel the chains weighing him down as he was once again thrown into the bilge. Re-living that time in 1574, kidnapped and held for ransom at the age of Twenty-five, by a woman, made him the joke of all of Ireland and England. No one let him forget it. He watched it all, as it was happening centuries ago.

Mick had planned his revenge well; he spent weeks laying in wait for Grace's ship. Captained by her son, the ship returned proudly with stolen East Indies cargo still in its hold. They were not expecting trouble this close to Ireland's shore, it was easy to board and transport the cargo, except for the flask he kept for himself; the flask he had thought would hold wine to help him celebrate his victory.

As he set the ship afire, and its crew overboard, he drank a toast from that special bottle. ...He soon realized it was not wine, as he tasted the bitter elixir that would change his life forever.

## Chapter 17

# Money to Leave

We were sitting in a booth at the back of the pub with a tall, cold pitcher of Guinness, on the table in front of us, when Mary and Simon came in. It must have been due to my shock that I didn't notice the glow that came from both of them, but Molly did.

"Well, now, it looks like a wee bit of fresh country air did you both a world of good indeed," she said.

Then I noticed Mary blush. Now, Mary never blushed very often, so I looked at Simon and he was grinning. Oh, there goes my helper, I thought.

Mary looked at the drink in front of me, sat down, and reached for my hand. "Okay, what happened? You seldom drink, so what's up? Did you lose your job or lose the tickets home? What's going on?" she said, concerned.

I laughed. "You will not believe it when I tell you, but here is the proof," I said, handing her a little savings account book from the Bank of Ireland building next door to the pub.

"OhmyyyyGawd! Where did this come from?" Mary yelled

and handed the savings book to Simon.

"Well, it seems that somehow the solicitor's office overlooked the fact that some cows were sold after my uncle died, and the money was placed in an account for me. The funny thing is, the deposit has today's date. The deposit must have been made this morning, *after* I asked to meet with the owner of the legal firm that handled my family's affairs and a lot of good that meeting did us. He didn't tell me any more about Maureen than I had already heard. 'She has not shown up for work and has been replaced.' Then he hands me this and tells me to have a good flight home. Do you believe this?"

"But, Bridget, there are ten thousand euro's here; did he say how many cows your uncle had?" Simon asked.

"No, he didn't go into details. He just had me sign something, showing that I was paid in full for 'property sold' in my name. I really don't understand any of this, but I was too shocked to ask him any questions."

I looked over to Mary, and she had a strange look on her face.

"Well, Mary, what do you think?"

"I think," she said with a smile at me and then at Simon, "that we go to the nearest church and light a candle to St. Patrick."

We all walked up to the top of the village and entered the beautiful church, named, appropriately, St. Patrick's. Simon stayed outside with Mick as Molly, Mary, and I said a prayer of thanks, and in my case, I also asked for guidance. We lit several candles and left a good-sized donation in the box for the poor.

When we came out, we decided to have fish and chips for dinner. We headed back down the hill to a small restaurant not far from the pub. During dinner, Mary told us of the discussion she had with Simon regarding the possible suspects and the need to obtain a search warrant for Killkeary Farm.

Simon had made some phone calls but still had no luck since he couldn't go into complete detail. He was needed in London to press his case since a 'search warrant was not to be obtained on a hunch,' as his supervisor informed him.

He also planned to see if Finnegan or Brennan had served in the military, and if so, what the details were. Mary planned to look into the land purchase, the development of the Knock airport, and its many board of directors members, to see if she could narrow it down to one potential suspect.

Since Simon would be flying from Knock to London, he loaned Mary his car. *God help him. I gathered he hadn't noticed how she drove*, I thought with a grin.

Mary and Molly planned to head back to Dublin in the morning. I looked under the table where Mick was hiding and devouring his fish and chips and announced that Mick and I would stay in the area and look around. This caused a bit of an uproar, but when the dust settled it was agreed that perhaps I could do some good poking around on my own, and Mary would join me in a couple of days. I dropped off Molly, while Mary drove Simon to the flat he had rented for the length of the investigation.

Mick wasn't allowed in the B&B so I made him a bed in the car, opened the windows and told him to behave. I had a funny feeling that Mary might be a little late in joining me so I went ahead and showered and got into my PJ's. I was reading a great book I found in Barbara's library called 'Angela's Ashes' when Mary finally showed up. She was humming when she came in and just smiled at me.

"Spill, I want all the details!"

She lay across her bed and said, "I really like him Bridge, isn't he great?"

"I can tell that, what happened after we left you guys alone?"

"Well, I cleared off the table and went to dump the remains in a nearby trash bin. The bin was on a short incline, and I must have slipped, for the next thing I knew I was on the ground."

"Did you hurt yourself?"

"Nope, but Simon rushed over and pulled me to my feet. He held me very close and without thinking, I placed my hand on his chest and looked into his eyes. Did you notice that he has eyes of liquid silver?"

She didn't wait for me to answer that and with a mooneye look on her face she continued.

"His look was so intense, rather than releasing me, as I expected, he held on tight. When he kissed me I stiffened for a moment, unsure of what I should do. My first instinct was to break his grip, but the feeling of his mouth on mine had a curiously numbing effect on my brain. Well I just had to kiss him back, didn't I? It seemed natural to continue moving into the kiss, and then we heard "Get a room!" shouted from of group of young hikers about to make the trek up the 765-meters of Croagh Patrick."

"Yuck, what rotten timing, what happened next?"

"Well I stopped kissing him and pulled a little away but I couldn't move very far. He laid his chin on the top of my head and I could hear, and feel, his heavy breathing."

"Holy cow!" I whispered. "That was some kiss!"

"Yup, a number 11 on the Richter scale. I didn't know how to tell him how delicious he was. I thought I heard him mumble, 'That was way out of line; I should not have done that.' And that felt like a splash of ice cold water and helped me pull my wits together. I put both hands on his chest, trying to pull back far enough to see his face so that I could understand. "I thought it was great, I asked him what he meant by *out of line.*"

"Well he is on an investigation and you might be a suspect," I suggested.

"That is what I thought and was getting ticked off when he said, 'I have wanted to kiss you in the worst way, ever since I first laid eyes on you, but we are in the middle of an investigation. I should have waited until it was bloody done with.'"

"What did you say?"

"Oh, I gave him the hundred watt smile and said, I don't think so. We make a good team . . . and we can't be working twenty-four-seven. Simon laughed, kissed the top of my head. He was going to turn away when I reached up and kissed him. Yup, Bridge, it's even better the second time."

I laughed at the standing test we have. Once may knock your socks off but can *they do it twice?*

"Bridge all I could think of was that I'm in so much trouble. I know we hafta leave in a few days, but I really don't want to leave this country or this man. I looked up at Croagh Patrick, and prayed for a little miracle. Then we get back and you got that money, can you believe it?"

"I wondered what prompted that sudden visit to church." I laughed.

"Hey you don't get a miracle that fast every day, 'gotta go out of your way to say a proper thank you' as Mom would say."

"What took you guys so long to get back?"

"Simon took his time driving back to Ballina. We made several stops along the way to see the sights, and discussed the possibility of Tom Brennan or Martin Finnegan being the murderer.

"I can't see Martin being anything else but a farmer," I said. "He sounds like a really great guy."

"That is what I think, although he does have a military way about him. Nothing he said, but with his erect posture and long-legged walk, he reminded me of one of those British soldiers you see marching in the movies. That could just be his style. He looks happy and makes do with the land he has. But what's incriminating is that I have a feeling he does know about the four hundred hectares you own."

"Both of those men may know about the land. The way that I see it, Tom and his family have much more to lose."

"That is what Simon thinks, he will try to get a search warrant, and perhaps we can see what's in those hidden files of Brennan's."

## Chapter 18

# Gravesite

Since I was planning to look around the area anyway, it was decided that I would drive Simon to Knock Airport. Molly and Mary headed to Dublin only after I promised to call them every night and right away if I needed their help.

After Simon boarded a small, twenty-passenger commuter plane for his trip to London, Mick and I walked around the airport. It wasn't very large; the terminal building itself was only the size of a three-bedroom, ranch-style home. I noticed that they had a car rental agency, which might come in handy if we needed to rent a second car.

There were a couple of private planes parked in front of hangers, and even an emergency helicopter. I had no idea what I was looking for. It all looked okay to me. According to Simon, this airport was receiving guns and explosives, which were being used in attacks against England. They knew that they were coming in by way of France, but after several attempts at stopping passengers, checking all the trucks and their deliveries that came from those flights, authorities still couldn't find a thing.

Mick and I looked around. All we could see seemed okay. Like what did I expect to find, a guy standing guard outside a hanger with a mask and an Uzi?

Disappointed and feeling so far out of my league, Mick and I went back to the car.

"Mick I want to visit my family's graveyard. I am sure it is around here somewhere."

I drove part of the way down the circular drive that was part of the main road into the airport, and I noticed a small dirt lane leading off to a wooded area. I slammed on the brakes and took that turn.

*"What the bloody hell?"* Mick shouted as he knocked his head on the front window.

"Sorry, Mick, I need to take this road, and I almost missed it. Anyway, you should be sitting back in your seat, instead of looking out the window with your paws on the dashboard."

Mick looked at me. *"Why do you want to take this old dirt road, Bridget?"*

"I want to see the family graveyard while no one is with me, and this is the way there."

Mick continued to look at me but didn't say anything else. I maneuvered the small car down the dirt road and around curves to another somewhat hidden road on the right, and finally we were there. I pulled as far off the road as I could and got out. There in the field alongside this unmarked road was a small private cemetery. There were only a dozen or so headstones, some very elaborate and some very plain, but all well cared for.

There were fresh flowers in front of the Carin plot and I wondered who had placed them there. The family headstone was about six feet of black granite with white lettering that told the sad story of my family.

Peter Carin buried in England; John Carin buried in the United States of America; Michael Carin buried in Australia, Joseph Carin buried in Italy; then the others, those who stayed home, who lived, worked, and suffered the hardships of farming in a much poorer Ireland than it was today. The grandparents I never knew, Anne and Patrick. My Uncle Patrick, Aunt Mary, and Aunt Winnie, family that I would love to have been around.

I knelt and prayed for them and asked their help in saving the land that they had all worked so hard for. I reached out and touched the headstone. Then it happened, I felt as if I had touched a power line, energy raced up my arm but I didn't pull away.

After a few minutes, I felt the familiar comfort that I had known as a small child. At night while dad was in the bars and I could hear the neighbors fighting, the police sirens and noise of the city, I would cry in fear and they would come. The quiet loving voices were there to protect me. I remember how it felt to be surrounded by the warmth of their love. I felt somewhat lightheaded as the memories rushed by. I closed my eyes and held my face in my hands. How could I forget, when did I lose the connection? These are the voices I have been hearing, not frightening but comforting and guiding.

After a few moments I began to see scenes play out, as if I were watching a slide show. I saw an old plow horse, attempting to plow a field of rocks. The old man handling the reins looked a lot like my dad. His arms strained with each move of the blades over the rock hard sod, his muscles bulged and the sweat poured freely down his face. I knew I was watching my uncle struggle to survive on the land I had inherited. I then went further back in time and watched as every member of the family tried in vain to dig up potatoes before they rotted in the ground. Through hundreds of scenes, I learned the strength of my family as they struggled to survive.

The Carin's had never become famous or had a great deal of money, but they took care of their family, friends, and neighbors. I realized that I had often thought of my family's shortcomings and all the things they didn't have, rather than the incredible strength they did. I thought of how difficult it must have been to leave the land and family they loved to struggle and survive in a strange land. I was filled with a sense of pride to be a member of this family.

I don't know how long I knelt at my family's gravesite. I heard a woman's voice telling me that this land was my birthright and that they all knew that I would not only meet, but overcome all challenges. I would not let them down. A female voice told me to *"remember the gifts you have and be open to let them work through you."*

Then I heard a strong male voice tell me, *"Take a walk across the land where your father worked and played and you will get the answers you seek."*

I looked around for Mick, and saw him sitting in the passenger seat of the car, just looking at me. His stance told me that he was guarding and protecting me. What a special gift he was.

It wasn't his voice I heard. I knew now that there were others with me on my journey. I'm not alone, I never was, but before coming to Ireland I never thought of the family, my family that died before I was born. They are of my blood, I have their blood in my veins, and they are a part of me. For the first time, I feel that I can do anything and that I will never have to do it alone.

I got back in the car, drove directly to the farm, and parked the car. I was ready to meet the tenant; I was ready to walk my father's land. My land!

"Okay, Miss Bridget, could you please tell me what the devil is going on with you?" Mick asked as I pulled in front of my barn.

"What do you mean?" I asked.

"What happened to the flibbertigibbet I had to teach to live in the moment? For starters, you did not know where the grave-yard was, yet you drove directly there. You, who can get lost at the drop of a hat, found your way from the graveyard, along unmarked back roads seldom traveled, to your family farm. You, who once looked as if a strong wind would blow you over, now look as solid as a mountain. You are beaming confidence all over the place. Right now I would say that you could take on the prob-lems of the world and come out a winner."

"Mick, I don't know if I will ever be able to do all the wonder-ful things you have taught me. I really appreciate the long hours you have spent with me each day. I don't know how, but somehow in the past week I have learned enough, and I now have some-thing I never thought I would ever have. It's not something that I could learn; I had to reach inside and give this gift to myself."

"And what would that be, m'dear Bridget?"

"Well, it's hard to explain, but for the first time I have hope. I know it sounds silly to you, since your role in life is that of a teacher, but I have not had a role other than survivor. Now for the first time in my life I believe that I will have a wonderful fu-ture. I have hope and a purpose."

"Bridget, 'tis no small thing you have been given. A great teacher once said that the single greatest advantage anyone can take into any battle is hope."

"I believe that. I now feel that I *can* keep my land in the family and I *can* solve the murder. I don't have to worry about the future, just like you said: do the very best that I can each and every day and tomorrow will take care of itself."

"Some way, somehow there is a plan for me. There is something I was born to do. If that's to be the next Sherlock Holmes, then I guess I'd better start learning how to do it right, for I plan on being the best darn detective there ever was.

"Let's go and find my so-called tenant. I wanna meet the guy that threw my mom's picture in cow poo. He will be so sorry he messed with an Irish woman from Brooklyn!"

Interlude

Grace could not control her temper as the memories of those dreadful days returned. "I was an immortal with full power. Many a great battle I fought with Morrigan and came out the winner, but now, even my appearance to mortals takes too much energy.

Her green eyes blazed as she looked at Mick's bowed head, "I vowed to get even, and back where I belonged. I had my ships search the world over for the wisest wizard to make a potion that would return me to full immortal power. I waited years! ...And an hour before my ship is to land with my potion, what happens? ...You drink it! You bloody eejit!" she shouted.

Grace sat back down, clearly exhausted by her emotional outburst. She took a deep breath, and continued in a much calmer voice. "I cared for my fae community but became bored. I found joy taking mortal form to become Grace O'Malley, the Private Queen of Ireland. Never did I realize that my cousin could kill my mortal form and condemn me to live out all of my days in spirit, as she took control of my faeire and set out to destroy the planet. For my husband Padraig, the faeire kingdom and the peace of the mortal world, I must regain my full powers.

"Mick, I need you to understand. Now, you and my wee Bridget are my only hope. I must regain my proper place. Do you realize the trouble that Morrigan is causing by instigating unrest all over the world? "

## Chapter 19

# Meet the Tenant

"Mick, what's wrong? Are you choking?" I asked as I pulled to the side of the road and turned off the car. "Mick, I don't know doggie CPR. Please tell me what to do."

"I am not *choking*, my girl, so stop fretting and please stop rubbing my neck. I was just a little overcome with merriment. Did you see the look on his face? I have never seen anyone turn that particular shade of *purple*." Again he started that choking noise, but this time I joined in the laughter.

"He sure was very nice at first, wasn't he, Mick? I don't know what I expected him to look like . . . maybe some swarthy-looking tall, thin villain, with a black mustache, not a short, muscled, young guy. I have to say one thing for him; he sure has the gift of gab. He looks more like a guy you would meet on Madison Avenue. He has that suave look about him. He was so smooth I was ready to sign the land over to him right there.

"Then when he asked when we were *leaving*, in that cocky way, it was as Mary would say: 'In the space of an instant, my senses shifted from dial-up to broadband,' and I remembered that this smooth-talking country gentleman was the guy who was in court trying to take over my family's land. He was the fellow responsible for the cows in my family home, and the person responsible for putting my family's possessions out in the dump pile to be destroyed.

"His complexion did change a bit," I chuckled, "when I told him that I was staying and that I would take him to the highest court in all of Ireland before I let him take my land. His color was so red it was almost purple and reached up to his scalp."

"I think the best part was when you told him that he could leave his cows in the pasture *for now*," Mick chuckled, "but you would give him notice when he had to move them... I also liked that you insisted he clean up the house and no longer use it as a barn."

"Well, we did find out what I wanted to know. Mr. Connor Claffey does have a quick temper, and I think that if I pushed him hard enough, he really would come after me. But I don't know, Mick," I continued, liking the idea that I could say my thoughts out loud in the privacy of the car so I could hear them and sort them into some sort of pattern. At least I hoped I could. "I still don't see Connor Claffey as a possible suspect. He is tough looking, a bully who likes to get his way, and has a quick temper, but I don't think he is very smart. I do have to say that there is something about him that gives me the creeps."

"Could be his squinty eyes?"

"Your right and that sneer of a smile didn't reach all the way to his eyes. Yuck! Barbara said that when he first moved here, he must have had some money. He bought a small place near my farm and grew his herd by so many cattle that he needed my uncle's land for them to graze on. He was also able to hire a good number of local guys to take care of it all. But he has no history here. How he could know of the four hundred hectares of land is beyond me.

"Could he have found the original land grant and is trying to get the forty hectare parcel first legally? But that doesn't seem possible, does it? He may have heard about it from someone local, but I don't see the locals giving out that information, do you?"

"Darn," I said as I jammed on the brakes. "I have so many thoughts running around in my head that I drove right past where Mary said she and Martin Finnegan walked the other day. Let's turn around and check out that place next. Ah forget about it—I have a better idea. It looked to me like Connor just started feeding the cows, so I wonder if I should go and talk with his wife now."

"Why would you want to do that?" Mick asked.

"Well, I'm not sure about Connor, but maybe I will get some vibes from his wife. She could be guilty also, couldn't she?"

We drove to a fairly new, small, ranch-style house around a curve in the road from the farm. There was no welcoming drive, just mud. It reminded me of pictures of trailer homes just plopped down for temporary housing. It was once a nice white house with black trim, but now it just looked sad and neglected. The front screen door hung on one hinge and had a large rip in the screening.

Mrs. Claffey didn't answer my knock for several minutes, and then I heard this squeaky quiet little voice whisper through the door, "Can I help you?"

"Hi, Mrs. Claffey, my name is Bridget. I hear that my Uncle Pat was a neighbor of yours. May I speak with you a moment?" I asked.

As she quietly, and cautiously, opened the door, I had a feeling that she had been told not to let anyone in, but curiosity, and manners, got the best of her.

"I am sorry that Mr. Claffey is not here to greet you, but he should be coming back soon," said this emaciated woman who stood before me. She was leaning on the doorframe as if it was holding her up. Her body was so thin that her housedress looked to be several sizes too large. I couldn't determine how old she was because she had her dirty black hair pulled straight in front of her face. I was looking at her so closely that I wasn't watching where I was walking, and almost tripped.

"I am so sorry about that. It is that man's traveling kit, and he won't hear of me moving it. He must have it at the doorstep for when he wants it," Mrs. Claffey said in the same strange little voice. I couldn't put my finger on it but something about her voice sounded very familiar.

"I'm sorry to disturb you Mrs. Claffey, but I . . ."

"Please come in and wait for him and please call me Helen," she interrupted.

"Helen," I said with a smile. "I just wanted to stop and meet you. I was hoping you could tell me a little of my family, if you have the time."

She looked up at the clock on the wall; it had been a half an hour since I spoke with her husband, and I wouldn't think it would take much longer to scatter hay. She probably thought so also. Helen turned quickly toward me again and then I saw her face.

Now I knew why I recognized her voice. I had volunteered at a women's shelter. I have heard hundreds of voices just like hers, and seen hundreds of battered faces. She was able to stand, luckier than many I had known. Both of her eyes were black, and one side of her face was still bright red. From the way she was leaning, I knew that not all of the bruises were visible. As if reading my thoughts, her body began to crumble in upon itself, and she sat down.

The door I mistook for the front door, must be the back door, or this was a strange house. The front door had opened to a large kitchen with a well-worn wooden table and six chairs. A large stove like that at Hillcrest dominated the room. I went over to the kettle that was boiling on the stove, and made her a cup of tea.

I started talking is a soothing tone. "Please just sit. I can see the kettle is at a boil, and I will just make you a cup of tea. I won't be able to join you today, I just realized that I really can't stay, but if it's okay with you, I will come again some other day. Perhaps earlier, when Mr. Claffey leaves, so we can have a nice talk," I said placing the large, cracked, brown, earthenware mug in front of her.

"Is it okay if I use your bathroom before I leave?" I asked, but didn't wait for a reply, as I rushed into the other room. Next to the kitchen were a living room and a hall leading to two bed-rooms. One bedroom had a large full-size bed with four large cherry wood posts. The bed matched the nightstands, vanity, and large dresser with a mirror that took up most of one wall. A large hope chest was at the foot of the bed in a lighter wood. I bet she brought this furniture set with her when she was married, I thought. *Hope chest— boy, is that rightly named.*

The only decorations were two large frames on the wall by the door. The picture must have been taken on their wedding day. In it, Helen looked sixteen and Connor many years older. They both were smiling. They were wearing very formal wedding clothes and standing by a horse-drawn carriage, with a grand mansion of a house in the background. Next to the picture was a framed copy of their wedding certificate. My eyes searched out the date right away. I almost yelped out loud. *Oh, my Gawd, that was only five years ago! Now she looks like a sixty-year-old, while Connor looks in his forties.*

I hurried back to the kitchen, and Helen was exactly where I had left her. Every instinct in my body called to grab her and get her out of that house of horrors, but I knew I had to wait. I had no idea what, if any, domestic violence laws were in place in Ireland.

"Sorry I have to rush off today, Helen, but I will be back soon. Would early morning be the best time?" I asked.

"Yes, that would be best," she whispered. "Some days he has a meeting with the man, but I seldom know when that will be."

I let myself out, and sat behind the wheel. For once I was very happy that Mick could read my mind, because I was in no mood to talk.

After seeing Helen, I needed some fresh air. I parked the car by the burial mound, and we walked from the mound to the main road, and there it was. A dirt road, a little hidden from view, but Mary was right. One had to know where it was, or to be looking for it; it wasn't easy to spot just driving by.

Not worrying about traffic, since I had seldom seen a car on this road, Mick and I crossed the two traffic lanes and walked down a narrow dirt road. The road climbed gradually and made a sharp turn about a half mile in.

"What on earth is that Mick?" I asked.

Mick responded in his full teacher mode. "At first glance, I would say it was what is called a ring fort, or rath. But upon closer inspection, I'd say that this one is called a cashels, a ring fort built of stone, usually situated on the summits of steep-sided rocky outcrops as this one is.

"You see here," Mick said, staring at the location of the fort, "that a considerable degree of natural defense is provided by the chosen situation. This one was certainly constructed in what seems to have been a deliberately defensive position. This great cliff-top fortress clearly has significance in military terms. With its triple walls, it demonstrates almost an obsession on the part of the long-dead inhabitants for maximum security and safety."

"Enough!" I shouted. "All you needed to say was that it was an old fort. Heck, we even have those in New York, but not this old."

I attempted to climb, but I guess sneakers and slippery rocks were not meant for each other. "Mick, I'm really curious about this place. Do you see any way in?"

"Not that I can see from where we are standing. Perhaps we would need to get to the top," he said.

"Well, I guess we have to pass on that for today. I had better go to the store and buy some hiking boots. Hmm, just what I need: a little shopping therapy," I said with a large grin.

"A little what?" Mick asked.

"Never mind Mick. You are a boy dog. You wouldn't understand," I laughed.

"Oh, but I do understand that you are not focusing on the task at hand."

We got back into the car, and I drove us back to Ballina. I stopped the car and asked a woman just about to cross the street where I could find the mall. She directed me to the town of Westport.

On the way there, Mick and I went over all the details we had learned so far, and we were still baffled. At that point, it looked as if everyone was a suspect. We had Tom Brennan with a total of two-hundred hectares and the most to lose if someone was to lay claim to his property.

"Martin loves the land and wouldn't want to see it changed. Connor Claffey, the tenant, was trying to take the land legally. Then we have the law firm, where there could be a solicitor who might have learned the truth from Maureen and had her silenced. They also may have paid me off with those ten thousand euro's to get me out of Ireland so they could claim the land.

"Heck, even the real estate agent said that he had had many conversations with Maureen about my land. He then offered me fifty thousand euro's for the 'small bit of bog land,' as he put it. And don't forget, we had a possible unknown person or persons at the Knock Airport."

We spent the entire trip to Westport going over and over the suspects to determine who would gain the most. I had always heard to follow the money, and that would lead you to the guilty party. Or was that just a TV Detective talking?

Soon we were driving up and down the streets of Westport, and for the life of me, I couldn't find a mall. I was getting really frustrated when I heard Mick making that choking noise again. "Okay Mick, what's so funny?" I asked.

"Make a right turn at the corner, find a parking place, and I will show you," said my laughing companion. I did as he directed.

"So what's up?"

Mick did his Pointer act again. "What do you see?"

"It's a picture-perfect scene of flowering trees, and a winding river leading to a large mansion," I answered.

"It is very beautiful. Some folks around these parts call it *the*

*Mall*," Mick said with that choking sound again. Between laughs, he went on to explain. "Bridget, that is Westport House, which was built on the site of an O'Malley Castle, and that, is the River Carrowbeg leading up to the front of the house. The Browne's, who came here from Sussex during the reign of Elizabeth I, even had the course of the river altered to make the Mall a grand approach to the gates of the house.

"There are some nice shops a few blocks over, and I will direct you, if you promise to park in a nice quiet spot so I can take a nap without tourists looking in the car windows and making kissy faces at me," Mick said.

I parked alongside the river, under the shade of a low-hanging cherry tree in full bloom. I told Mick I would only be a few minutes and left the window down in case he needed to visit a tree.

I came back about an hour later, only because I couldn't carry another thing.

"Did you leave anything in the shops?" Mick asked.

"Oh, I picked up a few things for me and Mary. I wish you had hands instead of paws. I need help," I said, dropping bags next to the passenger door. I finally found my car key and opened the door to place the bags in the trunk, or what they call the boot over here.

"I thought that you were just going to buy hiking boots?" Mick asked.

"That was the plan, but then I got to thinking that if the Garda and Scotland Yard's red tape is as bad as it is back home, then Simon will never get a search warrant. So I had to buy an all black outfit, and I even found black sneakers. With this outfit I look like a jewel thief. It's a blast, wait till you see it."

# Chapter 20

# Burglar

"Okay Mick, you remember what you need to do?"
"Sure I do, but I will caution you one more time, this is not advisable. The odds are against you pulling this off. You have no experience, there could be severe consequences if you get caught, and—"

"I know, I know, you have warned me for the past three hours, but I think this is the only way. I know Mary or Simon would never do it, and it must be done, so please be quiet so I can listen for the guards. Boy, I wish you could give me a lift up; hey, how strong is your back?"

"Don't even think about it," Mick silently growled at me.

With the information Mary gave us in her great report on the layout of the house and grounds, I had no problem finding my way to the stone wall, closest to the library.

"Hey, this is a pretty flower. What kind is it, Mick?"

"It is called wisteria. If you are silly enough to go through with this, you are in luck; it has strong vines that you can stand on to climb the wall."

I was getting cold feet about this whole idea, but Mick's term of 'silly enough' got to me and no way was I giving up now.

I had very little trouble climbing up the ten-foot-tall, wisteria-covered stone walls. With my new all-black outfit, I knew I couldn't be seen in the dark, but I wished that my new tool belt would stop making clanking noises. I thought I needed to take fewer things with me next time.

I made it to the top and had just started my descent when my foot got stuck; I bent over to try to get it loose, but I fell. Not all the way to the ground, due to the vine wrapped around my ankle, but I think my head was only inches from the ground. No matter how hard I tried, I couldn't reach my ankle.

I was hanging in the darkness like a Christmas ornament, suspended by a vine that burned into my ankle, when I heard a strange noise. Blackness was everywhere, an inky veil that made me disoriented and dizzy. I squeezed my eyes shut, and moved my hands a fraction of an inch upward on the vines, fearing that in the next second it was going to snap and I would land on my head.

What was that noise? It wasn't the guards. I could still hear them in the distance, but I couldn't make out their words. This was like someone breathing, like a panting . . . holy shit! *Mick, please help me!* I screamed in my head.

Standing only inches from my face were two large Doberman pinschers. One made a sound like a very quiet menacing growl from deep in its throat. I could feel their breath on my face, and the smell, *Oh, my Gawd, what do they feed these guys?* "Mick, please come quick!"

I pulled both hands free, and covered my face. I finally heard Mick, and he was saying "Come here, my pretty ladies," and then they were gone.

I got an adrenalin rush I never knew I possessed, bent double like a gymnast on a set of rings, and got my ankle lose. I ran so fast across the lawn that if the guards were watching, all they would have seen was a blur.

*Hey*, I thought, *maybe I'm on to something here*. I could produce the *Hounds of Hell* inspirational video for runners who want to grain more speed, complete with a Doberman. I could be a millionaire!

When I got to the window outside of the library, I was very surprised to find it opened. *Hmm, maybe someone was too warm earlier and forgot to close it.*

Using my newly-purchased penlight, I spent over an hour searching every inch of that room. I was disappointed that I didn't find any locked drawers; I really would've liked to try out my new mini tool kit.

Footsteps! Someone was there. I waited. The footsteps grew louder, and then stopped.

Whoever it was must have seen the light under the door. *Dang, why didn't I think to turn it off before this? Now what do I do? I can just imagine two burly guards carrying Uzis. I can't think of any way to sweet-talk myself out of this.* I dropped to my knees and slid under the desk. Thank God it was a large, ornate, old-fashioned desk with a big opening. I heard a scuffling noise, then nothing. No one attempted to enter the room. I wondered what had just happened, but was too scared to open the door.

I quickly put back all of the fake books. All I found were legal contracts, bank statements, and a lot of plans for future development. Everything looked okay to me, but then again I wasn't quite sure what I was looking for. A copy of the Garnaqugoue Land Grant would've been very nice, but no such luck. I snuck out of the building without incident.

I returned to where I left Mick and found him lying on the ground by the car. "Great, here I'm risking my life for the cause, and my big bad sidekick is taking a nap."

In response, I got the meanest growl I had heard from Mick. "Hmm, guess you don't wake up in a good mood do you? Well, let's go back to the bed-and-breakfast and I can get some sleep also."

I didn't sleep very well; I just kept tossing and turning. Finally I gave up trying to sleep and made myself another list. Taking out the list of suspects, I reviewed all the pros and cons for each person.

What did they each have to gain from taking over the land? The funny thing was that the whole idea of my owning any land was still unbelievable, but four hundred acres was a pipe dream. If anyone knew me, well, that's the problem—I guess they don't. They would know that I wouldn't fight anyone for my land.

If I could find a cousin, or some relative to take over the forty acres, which I was told was mine, that would be great. I'm not a farmer, and this is farmland. The people who have worked this land, who have been here for generations . . . this is their land, no matter what it says on any ancient deed.

Maybe I should sit down with these guys and tell them that. That might work, but if they didn't know of the land grant, then if I mention it, they might all start a legal war, and I couldn't afford that. I'll wait and just quietly go and turn the land over to the folks who have possession of it now. All except the killer, that is—so that means that I'm back to step one. I have to find out who killed Maureen, and if I stumble across a terrorist, I can turn them over to Simon. Of course I have to also stop from getting myself killed.

I worked and reworked my list for the next couple of hours. I made a plan, starting with a closer look at the fort and turf fields first thing the next day. With that decision, I was finally able to get to sleep.

"Padraig, she has done it this time, I can take no more. Do you hear me, Padraig? No more! She is suicidal!"

"Yes, My Lord, please tell me, what did our dear Miss Bridget do this time?" Padraig said, hiding his mirth as he watched Mick materialize back at Howth Castle, all six feet, six inches, showing his Celtic fighting heritage as he shouted and shook his fist in the air.

"First of all, she got it into her head to

play at being what she calls a cat burglar. Do you realize that I had to knock out and tie up no less than three guards, open a window, disarm a security system . . . and two female Dobermans decided that I was prime male dog flesh? I was so shocked I could not materialize; I ran a dozen miles or so to elude them. Then do I get a simple thank you? ...No! When she found me near death's door, do you know what she did? She accused me of napping. I have had it! No more, do you hear me? No more!"

Grace watched Mick as Padraig attempted to contain his laughter and could see excitement for life in his eyes and was pleased. For the first time in centuries,

Mick was no longer a bored, idle rich man of the world. He was glowing. His strong rugged features no longer looked like a mask of stone, in contrast to his gentle nature.

My plan is working very well, Grace thought and smiled. "My Lord, I think it is time we speak of what is Bridget's future and what she must learn to complete the tasks ahead. Please, come sit with us for awhile."

## Chapter 21

# The Fort

*Six in the morning! What on earth am I still doing awake?* Well I can't sleep, so I might as well go check out the fort. I put on another one of my new outfits: a heavy Irish cable knit sweater, jeans, heavy socks, and sturdy walking boots. I didn't know when I would wear those boots back home. They weighed a ton, but the salesclerk said that they were the very best for climbing.

I hooked my black nylon tool belt around my waist, making sure it contained the rope and climbing thingies, and especially the rock hammer. I wasn't planning on breaking open any rocks, but this might help me do some digging, and, anyway, it fit nicely in my handy dandy tool belt.

I quietly left the house. I would've loved a cup of tea, but I don't want to disturb anyone this early in the morning. *Gawd, I would die for a twenty-four-hour Dunkin Donuts right now.*

The car was where I had parked it last night, but no Mick. I walked all around the house, but there was no sign of him. I guessed he was out for a stroll; I wouldn't be gone that long. I was sure that he would be fine until I got back.

I drove back to the farm at a leisurely pace since there was no traffic at that hour of the morning. I found myself looking over miles of open land and rolling green hills. I had always loved reading Nora Roberts' books, especially when she described Ireland, *but even she missed the mark*. I guess that it's hard to describe the peace and beauty of this land.

I had read that the west of Ireland was probably the part with the richest remains of Celtic ancestors. This is the place where the old Celtic language and numerous legends and faerie tales survived. Watching the sun burn away the morning fog, I could believe it. This land inspired the imagination.

If I hadn't seen cars parked in the village, I wouldn't believe that folks drove in this quiet area. I drove down the quiet dirt road in front of the schoolhouse and past my farm. This time I didn't care if Mr. Claffey knew where I was going. I parked right in front of the fort.

This stone structure was built in the same manner as the stone fences, just one stone upon another. These stones were much larger than the flat, oval-shaped fence stones; these were more the size of concrete blocks, and where the fence stones were a light gray in color, these were black. Whether the black was the original color of the stone or it got that way over time, I didn't know. Over the years, dirt and plant life had settled between the cracks, making it blend in to the hillside. If not for the green plant life, that fort would be the thing of nightmares.

I walked around it for over thirty minutes, but I couldn't find where there was an opening, and I didn't even sense one like I had with the burial mound. *I wonder if it's on top.*

Using my handy new rock hammer as a pick, and stepping carefully on outcropping rocks, I made my way up about thirty feet to the top. After a couple of mishaps, I was happy to stand upright. The view from the top was so worth the climb. I could clearly see my farm, Martin Finnegan's small cottage, the small, one-room schoolhouse, and the airport. I knew Tom Brennan's place was over to the east, but it was behind the hill. I also couldn't see Claffey's home; it was in a valley on the other side of the schoolhouse.

I don't know how long I stood there marveling at the fact that I was viewing hundreds of acres of land, with only a few buildings, trees, stone fences, sheep, and cows. I did see an area about the size of a football field that wasn't far from the fort. It looked like it might be the turf field. I could see where part of it was dug up. *I wonder how many families depend on that turf for their fuel. Would they kill to keep it from a stranger?*

I looked around the rooftop area of the fort once more and still couldn't see any opening. That was strange. *Well, I might as well walk over to the turf fields.* I reached for my rock hammer and it slipped from my hands. When I reached down to get it, I noticed a large, flat rock. It had a round shape, like that of a manhole cover. *Hmm, I wonder . . .* I placed the hook of my hammer under the rock and pulled. It worked; it was lifting up.

When I got the rock cover all of the way up, I turned on my flashlight. I found that there were stone steps leading down. It was a spiral staircase, so I couldn't see much unless I climbed down. I lowered the rock cover to the ground, and moved it to the side so it wouldn't block my way back up.

When I started down, I realized that there might be snakes. No the story is that St. Patrick got rid of all of those, but there still could be other venomous crawly creatures like spiders, *yuck*. Maybe I should have waited for Mick, but so far so good. I hadn't even had to battle a spider web. Now that's strange, I thought. *Indiana Jones was always finding cobwebs; maybe this has been used more often than his archaeology digs, but by whom?*

At the bottom of the stairs was a long, narrow opening about six-feet wide and six-feet tall, again oddly clear of any cobwebs or creepy crawlies, that I could see at least. Thank goodness.

I walked about twenty feet and the entrance got wider. It was about twenty feet wide and the ceiling looked higher. Was I walking down hill? It didn't seem like I was.

I yelled when my light struck something white and creepy looking. But when I got up enough nerve to walk closer, I realized that I had entered a long tunnel.

It was awesome; from what I could see, it looked like a maze of caves propped up by huge limestone pillars, which was the white color that had had me spooked.

I must have walked a mile at least. I had made four turns to the right so that I wouldn't get lost in the maze. The next time I turned right, I couldn't believe my eyes. I really needed to get Mary and Simon down here with me. I was looking at a cavern that was over a thousand feet deep, and had several passages leading into it. There were massive stalagmites, stalactites, and more columns that decorated the room. I wished I had had more light. It was beautiful. Just like a palace created by nature and fit for a queen.

After enjoying the sight, I turned to begin my journey back to the opening. After an hour or so, I realized that I must have made a wrong turn. I was in an area now that wasn't an ancient tunnel carved by nature; it was a well-kept man-made tunnel that was showing recent use.

I retraced my steps to where I must have made the wrong

turn, and continued walking until I noticed a barely visible aperture of light coming from the entrance. I didn't realize that I was moving on an adrenalin rush, until I let out a large sigh of relief at seeing the light from the opening. It was so nice to see the way out of here. This fort or should I say ancient catacombs, are beautiful, but still scary.

Suddenly the light from the entrance was gone, and that whole area was in total darkness.

"Hey, open that back up!" I yelled and began running. I made it to the steps and up to the top, but no matter how hard I pushed and put my back to it, the large stone covering the opening, did not move an inch.

## Chapter 22

# Trapped

I yelled until I was hoarse, but no one came to remove the stone locking me inside the fort.

Could the wind have shut it? I asked myself hopefully, and stupidly. I guess I didn't want to face that fact that someone had purposely abandoned me when they knew I was in here.

*All right, I guess someone wants me dead.* All at once I began to feel the cold, and hear noises I didn't hear before. This was no longer an adventure; this was my worst nightmare, locked in a crypt, a dark, damp and a way too scary crypt.

No, stop that right now. This is not a spooky dark crypt, there are no dead bodies, *I hope*. I am locked in a cave, a *beautiful* cave, under a *beautiful* fort.

Okay, Bridget, no sense in sitting here just feeling sorry for yourself. What would Indiana Jones do? He would look for a way out. Think. There must be another opening, maybe at the end of that manmade tunnel I found. I will just keep walking," I said to myself.

I walked a short way past the point; I had turned back from

my wrong turn, and couldn't decide what to do. I was now looking at the entrance to three tunnels and had no idea which tunnel to take. While I was standing there trying to make up my mind, my flashlight died.

"What the heck?" I shouted. "*No freakin way!* I just bought this. This can't be happening."

This was no Energizer Bunny light. *Now what do I do?* All of a sudden I was back in the past, feeling overwhelmed with life, and feeling like a failure again. I told myself I should have known better; there was no way I could do this; hadn't I always failed with everything I'd ever tired?

All the negative programming passed through my mind. All the rotten comments that hurt so bad they were hard to forget, I was being flooded with them. I dropped to my knees and started crying. "I can't take anymore. I just can't do this."

Then I remembered the words from one of Mick's many lectures. "Who you were yesterday need not determine who you are now. You can be a new person and live a new life. We learn our lessons from the things we want to forget. You don't go into tomorrow lugging all the weight of past mistakes. If you have made a mistake, then all right, learn from it and forget it. Regardless of what life may bring you in the future, you can be victorious. Today is a new beginning!"

With 'today is a new beginning' ringing in my ears, I dried off my face with my sleeve and got back up. *Okay, you are smarter than they are, just think.* I stretched out both arms and waved them from in front of me, to the side, and back again. I didn't want to run into any stone walls, but I knew that I had to keep moving.

Each time my fingers brushed against the cold stone walls, I began to shiver. I felt as if I had walked for hours. I was so tired, and very thirsty. All of a sudden I tripped. I felt a sharp pain on my forehead and the blackness swallowed me. When I came to, I moaned, grimacing in pain. My body ached all over. I sat up, rubbed my head, and felt a lump about the size of a goose egg above my right eye.

*"Do not lose your courage,"* came to me in a sweet female voice. When I opened my eyes, I was staring at a sturdy wicker platform in front of me and wondered what on earth it was.

I was sitting on a thick yellow carpet, the color of bright daisies. I looked at the platform, which was eye level, and saw a winged person, about the size of a big cricket, dressed in a long dress in jet-black velvet. Her blue-black hair was weaved through with something green and silver. Around her were tiny pinpoints of light and the light was brilliantly white, like the lightning I once watched in Montana.

As I stared at the light in her hair it grew stronger and brighter until it filled the cave. I suddenly felt more relaxed. Having light around me really helped. Maybe it was the lump causing the illusion, but it felt great.

I could see that we were in another cathedral-sized cave filled with stalactites and stalagmites that were imbedded with crystals. There was light, but it didn't come from the ancient lanterns along the wall that could be lit if needed. This light was brighter than any that they could've provided. I noticed what looked like a glass of water, and reached for it, and finished it off in one quick drink. If it was water, it was the sweetest, best-tasting water I had ever had.

I looked closer to the platform, and now there was a group of small people. I'm not talking about little people; I'm talking very, *very* little people. Some were wearing old-fashioned Irish country work clothes, some in what looked like monk robes, and others were in modern dress, except miniature size.

They were all holding hands and moving around a stone. It looked familiar, like something I had seen a picture of, or maybe in a museum. It was black, cone-shaped with needle-like lacing or etchings embedded on the surface in what looked like gold. I think they were all talking at once. It sure sounded like they were speaking, but I couldn't quite make out what they were saying.

I felt heavy, sleepy, and unconcerned. *Do I have a concussion? If I do, I must stay awake.* But I felt so happy and sleepy. *What was in that water, is this a magic sleep? Wonder if Prince Charming will come along and give me a kiss. With my luck lately he would turn from a prince to a frog. What's that smell? Am I in a barn?* Somewhere far off I thought I heard a steady pounding, and the distant sound of engines, but I didn't hear cows.

One of the little people in the monk's outfit spun on his heels, pointed a finger, and bellowed.

"She be a gifted one. See us, do ye? Well, do ye believe it now? Well, lass, I know whom thou seekest, for thou seekest . . . therefore, seekest no further."

I looked straight at the little guy with the loud voice.

"If you don't mind, I'm going to lie down now and take a nap. It must be way past my bedtime, or this all has been a very strange dream, so I will just go back to sleep, and wake up home in Brooklyn."

I lay down on what felt like a soft downy rug that had been placed over a bed of hay with my hand a few inches from my face. I felt the air stirring, and the beautiful woman in black—or was that dark green?—velvet dress was there before me.

She was kneeling on my hand. In a beautiful clear voice, she said, "Please tell me all that there is to know about you, my young friend. For I must know why you have the sight."

Now that was a strange way of saying what I thought she was saying, but that didn't stop me from telling her of Mary winning the contest, meeting with Grace and Padraig, and everything that had happened up until that day.

I thought I heard a lot of talking when I mentioned meeting the queen of the faeries, but I was so tired. I just kept talking and answering her many questions. I thought it very funny that she asked me so many questions about Grace, and I realized that I was no longer feeling very relaxed.

I don't know how it was possible, but the feeling I had of relaxation had been replaced with unease so strong that I began to shiver. I looked around to discover why I was feeling frightened. Everything looked the same, but the little people were gone, and most of the light was now around the lady. I looked at her.

"What's your name?"

Gone was the gentle, sweet voice, as she answered my question in an angry tone. "My name is Morrigan. Of course you have heard of me."

"Ah . . . nope, sorry, I haven't," I answered.

In a flash of lightning, gone were any lingering feelings of peace. I stared at Morrigan as she began to change. Her black hair lost all of its shine and its tendrils looked more like snakes whirling around her head. The brilliant light that filled the cave was gone, all except for the beam of light that surrounded Morrigan, but that was no longer white. It had more of a reddish cast.

"I am of the Tuatha Dé Danann, and I defeated the Firbolg at the First Battle of Mag Tuireadh and the Fomorians at the Second Battle of Mag Tuireadh," she bellowed.

"Hey, I remember you now! Was that in the first or second *Star Wars* movie?"

I guess I got the movie wrong, because the ground began to shake and the wind gathered up loose rocks. The noise sounded like a fast train approaching. A loud crack and I felt something hit me. The light was totally gone now and the wind picked up, I could hear it howling. At least I hoped it was the wind howling and not the Banshees my grandmother use to warn us about. The Irish angel of death could appear as a little old woman with long flowing silvery gray hair, who sits and combs her hair out while she cry's and wails. When angered she becomes a wrinkled hag that fly's over your head as she wails and those ear piercing wails have been known to shatter glass. I wasn't about to open my eyes to see if it was her.

I guess Bat Woman would've fought back, but fight what? A smart woman would've run, but run where? I did the smartest thing I could think of. I covered my eyes and assumed the fetal position. The funny thing about facing imminent death is that it really snaps everything else into perspective.

"Oww, that hurts!" I cried out loud, although I don't think there was anyone left to hear. I could feel the pain, and it was getting worse. Thank goodness for my great new Irish sweater; it was keeping my back and arms from being cut to ribbons by those sharp, pointy rocks being hurled at me by this freaky wind storm.

I began to shake in fear. If I had had any air I would scream, but my lungs were aching for air, and I couldn't breathe. *I have had it, I give up. This was the end of my short-lived career as a great detective.*

Then I heard a male voice, the same guy that spoke to me earlier, who had said 'seekest no further.' Now he was saying, "Ye have met with the one great queen and failed. Ye shall not win. Seekest no further, for ye are among the dead. Lay ye down to your final rest now."

"What on earth are you saying, give up? You have got to be kidding me. I don't just give up. I'm a Yank, remember? It would take more than a few old rocks to make me give up," and I shouted my old standby: "Begone with ye now!" Thankfully, I no longer heard my negative thoughts. Although why my thoughts spoke in that strange accent was something else.

I kept my eyes closed, and the world looked better if I didn't have to see the swirling red light and see the rocks as they made their way to hit me. *God, I wish Mick were here now. What would he say about all this?* Then I heard him as clear as if he was standing next to me. One of his lectures had been on fear and how it stood for False Evidence Appearing Real. Could this be in my mind? I asked myself.

Ouch! I didn't think so, or how could it hurt so badly? He had also said, "Fear will move all positive energy away from you faster than good, positive, constructive thinking will move creative energy toward you."

I wanted good things to come to me, like the armed forces and some major painkillers, so I figured I had better start thinking smart.

"Okay let's try it. What could it hurt?" I said out loud.

"Ouch!" *Okay, don't use the word* hurt. *False Evidence Appearing Real! This is all a nightmare, and I will not accept it. I will not accept it.* I think that I repeated "I will not accept it" a thousand times, but I don't remember. I fell asleep or passed out. The jury is still out on that part. I must have been dreaming, because I was back in the basement with Papa Prendergast. We were playing hide and seek, and I had somehow gotten locked inside the large wooden hope chest. Papa was calling for me to yell out where I was hiding, and help would come for me.

I yelled as loud as I could with my mind since I had very little air left. "Help, I'm in the caves under the fort. Please come and find me!"

## Chapter 23

# Prince Charming

I woke to find that I was still in the caves under the fort. Mick was so close to me that I could feel his hot breath on my face. I closed my eyes and sighed.

"Bridget, are you okay? Can you stand?" Mick asked.

"No, I don't want to wake up yet. I was having the nicest dream. There really is a Prince Charming. He was holding me in his arms; they felt so warm and comforting. I just know that he was strong and handsome. Finally I found my prince, and he kissed me. Not on the lips, just my forehead to take away my pain. But we would've gotten to the lips, so let me go back to sleep, Mick, please?"

"Well, now, that sounds like a fine dream. It also sounds as if you are doing fine. What happened? Did you lose your way?" Mick asked, but didn't wait for my answer. "You can lie there a bit longer. Help is on the way. I think Mary called in the army."

I let out a sigh, and was about to close my eyes, when that odor hit me again. *Okay, time to be smart, think smart.*

"Oops, why is the room moving?" I asked Mick. I had stood

up slowly, only to feel a wave of pain. I also had some nausea and major dizziness. I sat back down.

"Be good lass, and for the love of Pete, stay still. Help is on the way," Mick advised again.

"I can't stay still. I have to find the cows."

"But, Bridget, there are no cows."

"No cows? Are you sure?"

"I have been around cows. I would recognize one if I saw one."

"Mick, can you find the source of that smell?"

"Oh, you mean the manure?"

"Yes, the cow manure. If there are no cows, what's causing it?"

Mick began to sniff and moved away from me, directly toward the far wall. I noticed that someone had lit the sconces' in the cavern walls, but I was too fuzzy to ask questions. It was a struggle to keep my eyes open for long.

"Mick, what have you found?" I asked anxiously.

"I have found that there are two sets of tracks, and both have cow manure mixed in with hay and mud. The tracks lead directly to the wall."

I tried to get up to check out the wall, but the room was still spinning and I had to sit down again. Then I saw it, just as if I was watching an old black and white movie in slow motion. A man wearing old work clothes was pushing a wheel barrow and another was walking alongside him. They were arguing, the man facing the wall was pressing a stone at eye level. The wall swung open and then Martin wheeled the barrow carrying the body of a young woman that must be Maureen into the opening, as the wall began to shut behind him the other man turned and ....

All of a sudden Mick began to bark.

"Mick what are you doing, what did I just see, are they still here? Why the doggie act? That loud barking hurts my head. Hush, they will hear you."

"Sorry, lass, help is on the way, but I thought it best to announce where they could find us. It is a maze down here," Mick explained.

Just when I heard my name called, all went dark.

## Chapter 24

# To Catch a Murderer

I was lying on a couch in Barbara's personal living room, with Mary, Simon, Mick, and Molly seated around me. I still felt a little disoriented, but it was good to be out of the caves.

"Are you sure you are up to talking about it now?" Molly asked.

"Sure," I answered. "But I still don't know anything about any terrorist or a body. Can you bring me up to date on that while I finish my tea, and then I will tell you my story?"

Mary came closer and sat on the floor facing me.

"Bridget, last night when Molly and I didn't hear from you, we called Barbara. She had not seen or heard from you, either. She knew that you had left early that morning, before breakfast, but she didn't know where you were going. We asked her to put a large note on your door, which you wouldn't miss, to call us, no matter what time it was when you came in.

"When we didn't get a call from you, we were really worried. I called Simon this morning, and he left right away to help in the search. Molly and I drove as fast as we could to get here, but we didn't know where you were, until Mick found us," Mary reported.

"Mick brought you to the fort?" I asked Mary.

"Well, not really. We just spotted him on the roof of the fort. I knew we would need help, so we called Simon at the airport, and he brought his team to the fort. I had a rough idea about where you might be. You see, ever since Martin was nice enough to show me around, but got so rattled when I asked questions about the fort, I've been curious . . . not only about his reaction, but why something so historic wasn't in any guidebooks. So I started to Google forts and caves and got some great stories."

Mary reached for the notebook and began to read. "Did you know that Knocknarea, which is not far from here, is a fabled mountain on which Queen Maeve is said to be buried? The mountain offers a spectacular view of Sligo Bay and five counties. And get this: could it be just a coincidence that there exists a prehistoric passage tomb, right above the caves, on the top of the hill? And you have a burial mound or tomb not far from the fort. Is that another coincidence? Hmm, I wonder who is buried there."

I groaned to myself. I thought I knew, but that was another little challenge that I didn't want to deal with right then.

"Another type of legend," Mary continued, "is a legend of secret connections to far away locations, as told in the diary of Gabriel Beranger, 1779."

She read to us from her notes. "The cave is said to connect with another that is in the County of Roscommon, twenty-four miles away, called the Hellmouth Door of Ireland. It's told and still believed today, that a woman in the County of Roscommon had an unruly calf, and could never get him home unless she was holding him by the tail. One day he tried to escape, and dragged the woman, into the Hellmouth Door. Unable to stop him, she ran after him, without letting go, and continued running until the next morning. She came out at Kishcorren, to her own amazement and that of the neighboring people."

"So from these stories, you concluded that there must be a cave around here, and I was trapped in it?" I asked Mary in amazement.

"Well, I sort of know you, and I figured that you wouldn't be playing tourist while we were doing research, and if Barbara or her neighbors didn't know where you were, then you weren't around where people could see you. So it stands to reason that you were in a building or cave."

"Good deduction, Dr. Watson," I said laughing. I turned to Simon. "How did you find the terrorist stockpile?"

"When we drove to the fort, Mick was on the top and seemed to be waiting for us. When we reached the top, he was digging around the opening. It took some doing to get the rocks that someone had placed over the opening moved, but once we did, we began to search the tunnels," Simon said modestly.

"You should have seen him, Bridget, he was great," Mary said, beaming in Simon's direction. "He delegated his men to move the rocks, and spread out through the tunnels to find you. When we found you, you were a little dazed. I was holding onto you, and you were rambling about cow poop, two sets of footprints and then told us to follow Mick. I told Simon what you said, and when we turned to Mick, he barked as if he understood the conversation and ran back and forth from us to the wall.

"When we saw the foot prints leading to the wall, it didn't take Simon long to find the mechanism to open it."

*I can't believe it*, I thought. Mary actually stopped talking, sighed, and gave a lovey-dovey, hero-worship look to Simon. *Good Grief!* I thought, *she has lost it big time.*

Finally, Mary continued with her report. "Behind the wall, we found Maureen in an alcove; her body was covered with stones. It really was a nice final resting place. Simon himself found the weapons."

"Tell her what you found, Simon," Mary asked.

Simon reached for his notebook and began to read.

*"A guy with a notebook, were these guys meant for each other or what?"* I silently asked Mick, *"Look at that—they both love taking notes."*

Mick just looked at both Mary and Simon, and then looked over to me. *"I think I see a doggie smile,"* I said.

Simon was reading from his report. "The following describes the weapons that were found in the cave beneath the fort of Garnaqugoue. They are thought to have been manufactured for use by terrorists."

He looked to Mary and explained. "Obviously, the more you can kill with a given weapon, in the shortest amount of time, and the ease in which it can be taken into the vicinity of your targets, the better the weapon for terrorism. Naturally, the weapon of choice by terrorists would be a nuclear weapon. This has not been a problem . . . yet. This is the largest haul to date for Interpol. We found guns and explosives, including two hundred 9 mm semiautomatic handguns. All are high velocity pistols readily available, small, and concealable."

He continued to read from his list and then explain to us non-military types.

"We also found six dozen 9 mm Uzi machine guns. These have a high rate of fire and have been available for many years.

One hundred AK-47 automatics, all high rate of fire, with large bullets, easy to come by for terrorists, very rugged, and don't need much care. Hand grenades that can be for normal use or as a booby trap; fragment bombs which kill in a twenty to thirty foot area, and injure up to eighty feet away.

"We also found some that were packaged and all ready for shipment, which included: booby traps all photo-cell triggered, or as a backup on a visible and easy to diffuse trap. The trembler-triggered booby traps are very common. Car bombs that were ready to use as simply a pipe bomb or explosive in the hood, trunk, or seat of a car, in some cases remotely actuated. Attacks on persons in the car are usually smaller, whereas in recent years, cars and trucks have been used to deliver a bomb to some site. These types of bombs have become much larger, equivalent to five hundred to one thousand pounds of dynamite.

"Walk-away bombs, those bombs that are left behind by a terrorist . . . such as a briefcase, or placed in the tank of a toilet. These are usually in very busy public places like department stores, railway stations, airports, etc, etc.

"The most interesting thing we found, information that we are not releasing to the public, is a wall bomb. We haven't seen them in many years. Surprisingly enough, the only time I heard of these was when the IRA used them over thirty years ago, and only a few people knew how to make them. These are packed explosives ready to be placed in a wall, and then the wall is re-plastered."

*"Yup, those two are meant for each other. Both are long-winded about things that interest them,"* I said to myself as I thought over all that Mary and Simon had said.

"Wow that's a lot of work, and an interesting report. Thank

you for sharing it," I said to Simon, trying my best to stifle a yawn. "Did you have time to get that military report on Martin Finnegan?"

"Yes. He never served, probably because he was the only child and fatherless, so he had to work the land. As far as records go, there is nothing showing that he ever left this area. He doesn't drive; neighbors do his shopping for him and take him to doctor's appointments."

They all started speaking at once. Only Mick was quiet as he watched me intently.

*"What did you see my girl?"* Mick asked

*"Well I remember seeing Martin, it was like a dream or a flashback to what may have happened in the cave."*

*"Tell me what you saw or felt?"* he asked.

I told Mick the details of what I had seen. *"Martin sure looks like the innocent farmer and yet I know he is the one who murdered Maureen. Mick, how am I to prove it, they will lock me up and throw away the key if I tell them of my dream and accuse two men without proof."*

*"Bridget, your gifts are beginning to rise to the surface of your awareness. Some faeries are endowed with a talent for detecting the psychical residue left behind by those who had inhabited a room. It seems that you can distinguish the type and strength of the various emotions embedded in the walls. But you are correct; many are not ready to believe in psychic gifts of any kind. Now just use your noggin, you will think of something,"* he said, tilting his head to one side.

I waited a few minutes until there was a lull in the excited conversation around me and said, "Simon, if you have a second, I have given this a lot of thought, and I have a couple of ideas I would like to share with you and get your opinion."

"Certainly, what is on your mind?"

"It was early morning on a school day when I was locked in the fort. If the person heard me drive by, he might have then walked to the fort, climbed to the top, noticed that the entrance was opened, moved that heavy slab to cover it, and then loaded all of those extra rocks to make sure I wasn't coming back out."

Simon nodded again, as if to say he was following what I was saying.

I continued. "I'm thinking that when that person climbed back down, they would be very tired." Again I received the nod.

"I think that they would be too tired to walk over the hills. Come to think of it, they may have walked on the road to get to the fort initially, because the grass was still wet from the morning mist."

Mary and Molly were looking at me with a puzzled look, but I think Simon knew where I was going with this.

"If you walk down the road, you pass the school house . . . and if you pass the school house at that hour of the morning, you are sure to have been seen by someone, a custodian opening the school, a teacher, or student."

I looked over at an excited Simon, and he said with a smile, "I am on it." He dialed his cell phone as he left the room.

"He is on what, Bridget?" Mary asked. "What was that all about?"

"Well, I think that our friendly farmer, Martin Finnegan, may be the mastermind behind the terrorist stockpile," I explained.

"No way!" Mary shouted. "How did you come up with that?"

This gift is still new, I'm not ready to be laughed at, Mick understood, but do I dare mention it to Mary and Molly?

"When I was walking in the tunnel (*in between tears of panic, self talk and dreamland, but I wasn't ready to talk of most of what happened down there yet,*) I noticed hay scattered about, as if someone had been hauling some in a cart and it dropped off. Now that could've been anyone, but I also smelled cow manure. Since there were no cows in the caves, then it must have come off of someone's work boots. We're dealing with at least three area farmers: Tom Brennan, Martin Finnegan, and Connor Claffey."

"From what I saw of Tom's home, the land he has developed, and his plans for all the future development, he is way too busy to do any farming himself, and he looks as if it has been a long time since he has done any physical work." Mary said.

"I remember, that was part of your report. Also Martin's house is near the school, and the hill is high enough that he could see whether a car turned onto the fort road. When Simon told us about the wall bomb that hadn't been used in thirty years, I just knew who was behind all of this. If you think about it, only Tom and Martin are the right age. If Simon calls Luke, I bet he will find that in his youth, Martin Finnegan was an explosives expert for the IRA.

"When they interview the people at the school and find out Martin was seen on the road, they will still not be able to arrest him or his accomplice because they have no hard evidence. That's where we come in; we have to help Interpol out."

"*Help Interpol?* Jesus, Mary, and Holy Joseph!" cried Molly. "Now what are you planning to do?"

"Oh no, Bridget, now what's up?" Mary asked and Mick shouted silently at the same time.

"Okay guys, don't worry. We're not going to do anything dangerous, hear me out," I begged. "First we hear from Simon. If he reports that it was Martin who was seen, I will ask him to arrange to have someone pick Martin up and transport him to Dublin for questioning. I know Simon can't prove anything yet, but if he threatens Martin with a long time in prison, for some pumped up charge, he might break and squeal on his partner." I explained.

"We know that Martin has his set routine and does not like to leave his land. But if he doesn't break, how do we know that his partner will?" asked Mary.

"Wife abusers don't stand up to men; Martin's partner will sing like a bird, and we will know all we need for them both to get a good long prison sentence," I answered.

"Wife abusers, you mean Connor Claffey?" asked Mary. "Now why do you think *he* is the partner?"

"If we just review what we know of Connor, it all fits. We know that he came to this area and made good very fast, with little farming background. He wasn't a landholder on the original four hundred hectares, but was fighting in the courts for the Carin land.

"According to his wife, he travels a great deal, so much so he keeps his pack next to their front door, ready to leave at a moment's notice. A little strange for a farmer, isn't it?" I asked, but continued talking.

"He had a neighbor whom he calls 'the man,' another way of saying 'the boss man.' It just makes sense to me, but I may be way off. We will see." I received a silent, but respectful, nod from both her and Molly and a lopsided grin from Mick.

"Secondly," I continued, "we need to ask Simon not to pick up Martin until dawn tomorrow, just at the start of feeding time. He also needs to make the arrest very public. Maybe he should ask a neighbor to come with him, to show him the way to Martin's farm. While Simon is busy doing that, we're going to see Mrs. Claffey, but for now, I'm going to my room to rest."

# Chapter 25

## To the Rescue

Before dawn the next morning, we slowly drove past Connor's house. I was feeling much better and had dressed up for the occasion. I felt so relieved that all of this is almost over, that I wore my favorite outfit: my short, gray, Ellen Tracy skirt and white top, with my new Jimmy Choo Tress heels with off-black nylons, all topped off with my favorite Evan Picone black and red cardigan. I thought I was wearing the perfect outfit to go visiting. Mary was dressed in her favorite outfit also: jeans, fleece jacket, and well-worn Nikes.

"This isn't going to work. There is no place to hide the car." I turned to Molly. "Molly, would you just drop Mary and me off, and we will hide in the bushes until he leaves?"

"Sure thing," said Molly, as I pulled to the side of the road to let her behind the steering wheel. "Please just drive around, and pick us up at the school house in about an hour," I said.

"Mick, please stay with Molly. We will be fine," I assured him as he started to follow us. He didn't like it, but he stayed in the car.

We barely had time to get to the tall bushes that grew wild on the side of Connor's house, when the door opened. I heard Mary gasp, and she almost dropped the large shopping bag she was carrying.

"Shush, be quiet. I don't think he can see us, just be real still," I advised Mary.

We watched as Connor got into a small truck and drove out the driveway. We both gasped when he suddenly stopped the truck a few feet from where we were hiding. What I saw sitting on Connor's shoulder and whispering in his ear shocked me so much that I stepped back deeper into the bushes and pulled Mary in with me.

We could hear his cell phone ringing. He answered.

"Sure, I will see you soon. You worry too much. Let me set the boys to working, and I will be there." Connor looked at the phone and hung up. He just sat there a few seconds longer, as the faerie on his shoulder spoke to him.

*I think that this is one of those faeries that are up to no good!* I looked at Connor's sidekick and said, *"Be gone with ye now!"* and just like in Sandingham this one disappeared in a burst of sparkles. *"And I don't have to wiggle my nose or wear a pointed hat,"* I giggled to myself. *I'm glad that I told Mick about the first faerie; he assured me that I was just removing them to someplace I can't pronounce but I think it's sort of a purgatory or holding cell until things got sorted out. He never explained what "things" but at least the thought of a holding cell felt better than the thought that I may be destroying them.*

Connor shook his head and started driving again. This time he drove the rest of the way out of the drive, onto the road in the direction of the farm.

When the truck was out of sight I went to join Mary, and

I realized that I was stuck. "Mary, wait," I called. "I think my sweater is stuck in the bushes."

Mary put her bag on the ground. "Hold still; moving is just making it worse. You are really snagged." After a few minutes of struggle, she had me free.

I kept pulling leaves off my sweater and from my hair as we raced across the mud pit that should have been a lawn, and knocked on the door. This time Helen answered right away. She looked a little stronger, but her bruised face looked worse. The swelling had gone down, but her face was vivid shades of black, yellow, and blue.

The first thing I did was hug Helen. "If Connor does not come home again, is there a place you could stay?" I asked.

"He has a meeting with the man after the cattle have been feed, but he will be back, and I cannot leave. He will follow, and find me again," Helen said glumly.

Mary broke in and asked, "How long do we have before he returns from feeding the cows?"

"It usually takes a few hours; he feeds the cattle with his two helpers, and they have a few drinks. But today he has a meeting, and will be gone even longer. Would you both like a cup of tea?"

"Sorry, Helen, there is no time right now. Mary, please go take care of the backpack," I said, pointing to it in the front entrance hall.

"Helen, I have something to tell you," I said leading her to a kitchen chair. I told her of my suspicions, what I thought was about to happen, and the outcome I was counting on.

She looked dumbfounded. "Are you certain?" she asked hopefully.

"Well, not 100 percent, but I can usually read people and this feels right,"

"I should not be surprised by the bombings, for I know he is evil, but I had no idea his hatred of the Irish and English was so great. I will be glad to see the back of him once and for all. I don't know what to say," Helen said as she held her hands on her lap and rocked to comfort herself.

I handed her an envelope. "I want you to have this. Is there someplace you could go that's far away from here, just in case I'm wrong about his getting caught?"

At first I thought that she wasn't going to answer me, but she looked inside the envelope, and finally said in a hushed voice, "I have a good friend . . . well, we used to be good friends. She lives in Italy. I could stay with her." Then in a stronger voice, "I would love to get away from here. But I will not accept your charity."

"There you are wrong, Helen, this is not charity. I'd expect you to pay it forward."

"What do you mean by 'pay it forward'?"

"Something I learned from watching Oprah Winfrey, I don't want you to pay me back; instead, someday, if you can help another person with money or time, I would like you to help them, and in that way you are paying me back. Be sure to ask them to do the same," I said, smiling as I reached over to hold her hands. "You can get away, and I will be happy to help."

Helen started to cry and began to reach for me when we heard the sound of Connor's truck returning.

"Oh, my Gawd, it's him!" yelled Mary. "What do we do? Where do we go now?"

"Helen," I asked. "Is there another door?"

"No," she said. "He has it blocked, but you can go out the

bedroom window and across the creek."

"Okay, Mary let's go. Helen please be sure to act normal, and don't say anything. He must have heard they arrested Martin and is coming for his backpack. Just hang on a few more minutes."

Somehow I was able to hike up my skirt and slide out the window, but I landed face down in the mud.

Mary grabbed my arm and whispered, "Hurry, he may have heard us!"

As if I was lying in that evil smelling mud by choice. I got up and ran as fast as a well-dressed New-Yorker, in three-inch Jimmy Choo heels, covered in mud, could.

We reached the creek. "There is no way I'm getting my new shoes any wetter. There is a slim chance I can still save my shoes from mud, but water is another matter." I whispered.

I searched the creek for a way across the four feet of trickling water. "Oh, look, there are flat stones. I can walk across them," I said and proceeded across.

Just as I felt myself sinking up past my ankles, I heard Mary yell, "Don't step on those—they aren't stones. Those are *cow patties*."

By the time I walked the two miles to the school in cow poop shoes to meet Aunt Molly and Mick, Mary had finally stopped laughing.

---

"Mick, I can still *hear* you," I said. "Hang your head out the window farther, and you won't smell my shoes."

We were racing toward the bed-and-breakfast so fast I thought the car was going to take flight. I knew all the cows we passed wouldn't give milk that day, because of the fright of seeing a car driven by, at breakneck speed, with a dog and two women hanging out the windows. I drove but did have a little trouble seeing, since the smell was bringing tears to my eyes.

After a bath and a whole bottle of Neutrogena sesame oil, I felt really good about our getaway. We were all sitting in Barbara's kitchen having lunch, when in rushed a very tired and disappointed Simon.

Always the perfect hostess, Barbara jumped up and set Simon a place at the table and poured him a cup of tea.

"How did it go?" asked Mary.

"Well, we have Martin, but we just missed his partner. He left from Knock Airport where his friend had a plane; the friend is innocent, he thought that Connor had a family emergency. He took him to Heathrow where he was to rent a car. My people checked all of the car rental agencies; there was no one of his description renting a vehicle today," Simon answered.

"You were right Bridget" he said nodding to me. "When the Garda interviewed Martin, he gave up Connor as the terrorist we have been searching for. Connor is the legman and Martin is the planner."

"The folks in town will not believe this of Martin! Did he give any reason?" Molly asked Simon.

"It seems that Maureen had stopped by to visit him and mentioned that Bridget believed the land should go to one of her relatives who lived in Ireland so it would always stay in the family. Maureen asked Martin about the Carin family, and if he knew of any living relatives. It happens he does know a Carin cousin that lives in England, but he was afraid that, being from London, he wouldn't want to live in the Irish countryside; rather he would want to sell off the land to an English developer. He couldn't let that happen. He and his family had fought the English for so many generations. He had a great fear of losing the land. The fear drove him to kill Maureen in the hopes that the rich American would soon forget about the land in Ireland." Simon concluded.

Embarrassed about how close to the truth that was, if not for winning the airlines ticket, I would've forgotten. I asked, "How could someone have so much hatred and fear?"

"It would appear that most of the Finnegan clan had died on the Sandingham ships. Those few left alive made sure that the hatred was passed down."

"We have to be taught to hate," Molly said. "It 'tis a shame about Connor as well."

"How is his wife taking all of this?" Simon asked.

"Actually, she is still in shock that her living nightmare may soon be over. As soon as she heals, she will be joining her friend in Italy. Right now she is staying with Molly's daughter Evelyn in Dublin. She feels much safer out of Mayo until we catch her husband."

"Oh, by the way, Simon," I said with a smile. "We didn't think Connor was going to rent a car. Helen said he had family in France and went there often. We thought he might take the next flight to Paris, so we called a guy we met."

"So why are you all looking so cheerful?" Simon asked. We all smiled as I handed Simon a card. "What's this? Who is Charlie Boyle?"

"I forgot to mention that Charlie called here a few minutes ago to let me know they arrested a man fitting Connor Chaffey's description. It seems he was detained at the airport for carrying what looked to be two homemade bombs. When searching him they also found several passports under different names. Right now they are searching his Paris and London apartments for the addresses of his contacts."

"I wonder if they will give us back our cookie tins and curling iron," said Mary, and we all laughed at the puzzled look on Simon's face.

## Chapter 26

# Off to London

"I am so sorry to see you leave," said Molly as we packed up the car to drive to the airport.

"You will see us again real soon; London is not very far away." Mary said. "I still can't believe how everything is coming together for us. Simon has a friend who is on assignment overseas and he has left a flat in Battersea. We can stay there rent-free for a couple of months, until he comes home. And my company has a branch office in London that I can work from only a short train ride away."

"I am so happy for you girls," Molly said with a smile.

"Bridget will be busy finding her cousin to take over the land," Mary continued, "but thanks to the money from the sale of the Carin cattle, she will be okay for a long time without a full-time job. We were even able to sublet our apartment in Brooklyn. It's like it was meant for us to be here." Mary laughed, as she hugged Molly.

"I will not be the only one to miss you both," Molly said, as she looked over to where I was saying good-bye to Mick.

"I still can't believe all that's happened, but I know that I will miss you," I said, as I hugged Mick.

"Not to worry, your job now is to rest and enjoy London. We will meet up again very soon. You have learned a great deal, but there is still a great deal to learn."

I was so happy to hear that I would see him again that I hugged him even tighter.

"Please give a dog some air!" He grumbled. "Just be sure to call out for me, if you need me before we meet up. I will be there for you as soon as I can."

"You will? I mean, can you do that? Will you be able to find me if I need you? Hey, it took you a long time to come to the old fort."

"Well, I am sorry about that. I was in the middle of a discussion and not, as you say, tuned in. But I will be from now on!"

"That is so great! You are a super puppy after all," I said, as I hugged him even tighter, and this time Mick didn't complain.

When we finished loading the car and waving good-bye, Mick asked, "I forgot to inquire the name of that lady you met while you were in the cave. Was it the spirit of the woman in the story that Mary read to us?"

"I don't remember very much, there were several little folks, and one started out little then grew to full height. She asked a lot of questions, said she was very happy to meet me. Her name was Morrigan, and she said I would be hearing from her again, but I hope I don't. She wasn't very friendly."

Mick was silent so I said to Mary, "well, we had better get going," we both hugged Molly and Mick again, waved good-bye and drove off, joining the busy Dublin traffic.

# Interlude

Molly was smiling as she watched her niece leave. She looked over and was surprised to see Mick in human form. "Mick what is wrong, what did she say to cause you to materialize, she could have seen you."

"She met Morrigan in the cave."

"Dear God, what are you saying? Please tell me that she did not meet Morrigan of the Tuatha Dé Danann."

"Yes, I am afraid she did, Molly."

"Our Bridget met Morrigan, the Great Goddess of War herself, and she lived to tell about it? How is that possible? You said that Grace thought she could keep Bridget a secret from her old nemesis until she was ready? She is very far from being ready to take on Morrigan." Molly cried.

"How well I know. I guess we had better get Bridget ready very quickly."

"Are you going with her to London?"

"No, not yet, she should come to no harm on her own for a few days. I need to meet with Padraig and Herself to see what needs to be done now to speed up her training."

# About the Author

Bernadette Crepeau's parents originally came from Ireland and settled in Brooklyn, New York.

Bernadette now lives in Oregon with her husband and extended family, including two very spoiled dogs that have no communication problems. She is currently working on Book Two of The Leprechaun Trilogy. Turn the page for a sneek peak of what's in store for Mick and Bridget.

Bernadette would love to hear from you. Please send your emails to bcrepeau4551@comcast.net

# The London Leprechaun
## Coming June 2010

By Bernadette Crepeau

"What is this you are telling me? How on earth did you get into so much trouble in just one week? I spoke with you every day," asked a not too happy Mick.

"You asked if I was doing okay, and I am, well, sort of. You asked, whenever you called.... And how did you do that anyway, speak to me long distance like that? Do you need an extra brain chip or something for long distance? That's just plain *awesome*."

Mick didn't answer, so I continued explaining.

"Well anyway. When you asked, if I was seeing the sights, I told you I was. When you asked, where I had been, I told you: Buckingham Palace, St. Paul's Cathedral, the *family home* of the Queen and..."

"True." Mick interrupted, "But somehow, *you neglected* to tell me that the reason you were in St. Paul's Cathedral was that you found your English cousin. Who just so happens to believe that you are destined to join him in stopping an ancient evil organization from *destroying the Cathedral?*"

"Well, it's not like I have done anything about *that* yet."

"But you *plan to?*" screeched Mick.

"Hey, don't screech at my friend," demanded Q-tip.

Ignoring her, Mick continued "You also *neglected to mention* this young lady here, a teenage hoodlum if ever I saw one."

"Hey watch it buddy! I may be small but I have friends in high places." Q-tip said, as she flew a few inches above Mick's eyes. Her little body shaking as she confronted a dog, a hundred times her size. She was pointing her finger at him and the large head of white, cotton ball looking hair, from which she received her nickname, was shaking from side to side.

"Oh, pardon me, Miss Ear Wax is it? How did you talk Bridget into this scheme that has her locked in an ancient priest hole? A priest hole, that is about to be knocked down by a bloody wrecking ball?"

"Mick, I never said she talked me into it. If you would only listen. Hey practice what you have been teaching me, okay? Take a deep breath…

"*Q-tip* is a teenage Faeire, which of course, is why she can hear you speak. Q-Tip is not affected by Morrigan, no one, under what she calls, the age of reasoning… whatever that is, is affected. She is going to help me take down Morrigan. But before she does, she wants me to come and speak with her group."

"Help you do *what?*" screeched Mick.

"Yeah, like you don't know. When were you and my old greats going to let me in on the game plan? Noooooooooo, I had to hear it from a stranger. I shouldn't be speaking with you, but I do need your help in getting out of here, and *like soon* please. I can hear that wrecking ball. It's getting closer."

I could see that Mick was ready to argue some more, so I

interrupted before he got going again.

"It was Friar Xavier that actually got me here. Well him and Antoinette. Except Antoinette cannot see the Friar, since he is the ghost that watches over the royal family. Funny how I can see him, I guess I can do all sorts of things I don't know about yet."

I heard a low doggie growl and talked a little faster.

"Well, you see the Queen raises Corgi's, and she had bred them with Dachshunds. Now she is the proud owner of a new breed called Dorgis. Except someone has *dog napped the puppies*! Antoinette was caring for them and she is French.

"The papers are blaming the French people. *It's a mess.* So I was just investigating, when Q-tip and I discovered this place and we got locked in."

The sound of large machinery was almost on top of us. Pieces of rock began to follow the dirt and sand that had been coming down.

"Mick, can you get us out......like *now*!" I shouted.